RITA

&

Los Angeles

Bilingual Press/Editorial Bilingüe

General Editor
   Gary D. Keller

Managing Editor
   Karen S. Van Hooft

Associate Editors
   Ann Waggoner Aken
   Theresa Hannon

Assistant Editor
   Linda St. George Thurston

Editorial Consultants
   David Koen
   Ingrid Muller

Editorial Board
   Juan Goytisolo
   Francisco Jiménez
   Eduardo Rivera
   Mario Vargas Llosa

Address:
Bilingual Review/Press
Hispanic Research Center
Arizona State University
Box 872702
Tempe, Arizona 85287-2702
(602) 965-3867

RITA

&

Los Angeles

Leo Romero

Bilingual Press/Editorial Bilingüe

TEMPE, ARIZONA

ISBN 0-927534-44-4

Library of Congress Cataloging-in-Publication Data

Romero, Leo.
    Rita and Los Angeles / by Leo Romero.
        p. cm.
    ISBN 0-927534-44-4 (pbk.)
      1. New Mexico—Social life and customs—Fiction.
2. California—Social life and customs—Fiction. 3. Hispanic
Americans—Social life and customs—Fiction. I. Title.
PS3568.05644R58   1995
813'.54—dc20   95-1032
                                                  CIP

PRINTED IN THE UNITED STATES OF AMERICA

Cover design by Bidlack Creative Services

Back cover photo by Elizabeth Cook

Acknowledgments

Partial funding provided by the Arizona Commission on the Arts
through appropriations from the Arizona State Legislature; additional
funding provided by a grant from the National Endowment for the
Arts in Washington, D.C., a Federal agency.

The story "Pito" is based on poems that first appeared in *The
Americas Review* (Houston: Arte Público Press).

✧ CONTENTS

For Elizabeth

✧ Rita and Los Angeles

1

Rita knew Los Angeles before the freeways.

I can't imagine it.

Rita is what my mother had me call her from as early as I can remember. In fact, I don't ever remember calling her Mother. Margarita was her full name, but only relatives called her by that name except for her only brother, my uncle Necio, who called her Rita. She loved her brother, and he likewise loved her, so we saw him all the time. But she hated her five sisters who we almost never saw even though they all lived in Los Angeles. I don't think Uncle Necio saw them much more than we did. If he did, he never said anything about it.

Rita's first marriage only lasted about a year, but I always heard her speak of that year in Bunker Hill as if it were the best year of her life. It didn't have anything to do with her husband who she soon realized was not the right man for her. Mr. Fante is who she spoke about when she remembered her Bunker Hill days.

Rita wasn't even seventeen when she got married the first time. "Too young and dumb about the world and men," she often said, referring to herself back then. She was in her late twenties when she married my father. But that marriage didn't turn out much better, except I was born. He left us when I was ten months old. And as far as I know, he never tried to contact us and seemed to have disappeared from the face of the earth just like her first husband. "Good riddance," is what Rita had to say about the men who had been in her life. Of course that didn't include Uncle Necio who was three years older than her and had always been her protector. Nevertheless, even with all her bad luck with men, she kept finding new ones to date.

Rita rarely talked about my father and the time they lived together, but she frequently talked about living in Bunker Hill. She only mentioned her first husband to say that he married her and left her. When I was young and Rita would start reminiscing about Bunker Hill, I would block out everything else she said and think of the Korean War.

I was born shortly after the Korean War ended, and I grew up reading comic books about that war. I read about battles for hills with unusual names like Porkchop Hill and I think even Hamburger Hill, though I may be wrong about that. Anyway, a lot of hills with funny names. And so whenever Rita said Bunker Hill, I immediately thought of the Korean War.

One day the neighborhood kids were talking about their fathers or uncles who had fought in the Korean War. I proudly boasted that my mother (when Rita wasn't around I did call her Mother) had fought on Bunker Hill for almost a year. Seeing the incredulity on the kids' faces I got carried away and added that I was born on Bunker Hill in the midst of battle. The younger kids believed me, but the older kids immediately challenged my story. They said I was lying, that women weren't allowed to fight in the Korean War or any wars, period. I countered that she always talked about it, so it had to be true. All the time the older kids were laughing at me. "Don't you know Bunker Hill is in Los Angeles, stupid?" they said before running off and leaving me with the younger kids who were giving me dirty looks.

Even though the older kids said Bunker Hill was in Los Angeles, I didn't believe them until one day Rita and her latest boyfriend took me on a drive through Bunker Hill. Usually she didn't take me on her dates, but that day she was feeling especially happy, and she scooped me up in her arms, well not exactly, but as much as a small and thin but strong woman can scoop up an eight- or nine-year-old boy. "We're going to Bunker Hill," she said, and she said it as if Bunker Hill were a wonderful place where every other house was a store that sold ice cream and candy and toys.

"Bunker Hill!?" I said, and the words almost caught in my throat. If she had said we were going to the moon, I wouldn't have been more surprised. I imagined an incredibly long, narrow road across the Pacific Ocean. I had seen the ocean many times from Santa Monica and other beaches, and each time I saw it I couldn't help feeling some anxiety about there being so much water running loose outside the confines of pipes and swimming pools. Thinking of driving to Korea, I thought of the violent seas I had seen in movies. Couldn't a gigantic wave knock us off the road or break the road in two sending us to the bottom of the ocean? That was what was on my mind when I reminded Rita that we had forgotten to bring along life jackets and an inflatable raft.

She laughed at what I said, which was her way of dismissing any of my behavior she didn't understand. But her boyfriend stared at me in the rearview mirror as if he had just noticed me for the first time and was wondering if I was for real. It was the same look all her boyfriends gave me if they were around long enough to spend any time with me. I don't think they could ever see being my father, which was fine with me because I could never see any of them being my father either. And I was always relieved when Rita's relationships came to an end, because there would follow several months in which she would stay away from men, except of course for Uncle Necio, and Uncle Necio and her and I would do all kinds of fun things like going to movies and bowling and amusement parks.

You can imagine how disappointed I was when we arrived in Bunker Hill. I thought we'd be on the road for weeks if not months, and I was wondering how the filling stations and motels and restaurants would keep from sinking into the ocean. My head was filled with all sorts of images from G.I. Joe-type comic books about the Korean War, but that was all dispelled when Rita said, "This is it, Bunker Hill! Isn't it beautiful!"

Where we lived wasn't great but it was a vast improvement over what I saw out the car window, a neighborhood long in decline. How could Rita call it beautiful? I was too disappointed to say anything.

"That's where I lived! And Mr. Fante lived a few doors down. You see, where that broken window is. I'm sure of it even though I haven't been here in ages." Rita was barely able to contain her excitement as she pointed out a run-down building as if it were some world famous shrine.

"Fante?" her boyfriend growled. I could see this relationship was going to be shorter than normal. At least that was one bright spot in an otherwise bleak day.

"He was a writer. I don't know if he became famous." Rita was craning her neck to look back at the building.

"He couldn't have become too famous if you haven't heard anything," the boyfriend said with increasing impatience. First there was me on the date, and now this. I could read his mind. Who couldn't?

I half listened to Rita as she went on at length about her favorite subject: Mr. Fante the struggling writer. I had heard it countless times before, but I had never really listened. I had been hearing what I wanted to hear, a story about the Korean War she never told. Rita interrupted her Fante reminiscence long enough to tell her boyfriend to turn around and drive by the building again. I was beginning to feel angry over how cheated I felt that we weren't going to Korea. And then I cringed remembering the older kids in the neighborhood saying, "Bunker Hill is in Los Angeles, stupid." How could I ever face any of the kids again?

I had lost track of Rita's story by the time she turned around to look at me in the back seat and gravely announced, "Mr. Fante could have been your father." This was news to me and startled her boyfriend so much that he nearly sideswiped a parked car.

"Huh?" we both said at the same time.

As if the aborted Korea trip hadn't confused me enough, now there was this to deal with.

"Mr. Fante was my neighbor. Oh, you've heard me talk about this a lot," she said looking at me.

"I haven't," her boyfriend almost shouted. I was glad he said it because I wanted Rita to explain, but I didn't want to tell her I hadn't been listening to her all these years. We passed the building again, and Rita cast a glance at it, but what she was thinking about was of more interest to her than the building.

"Well, it'll bore Michael (that's me), but, anyway, Mr. Fante had a big crush on me. I'm sure of it. When my husband was off working I'd hear Mr. Fante clacking away at his typewriter. I'd hear it all day and all night. He'd type by an open window. And I noticed every time I passed by his window, he'd stop typing, and he'd start typing again when I was out of sight. One day I was trying to open my door while I was holding a bag of groceries. He happened to come out of his apartment at that time, and he rushed over to help me. I invited him in for a coke. And that's when I learned that his name was Mr. Fante. Actually he was only a few years older than me. But I liked to think of him as *Mr.* Fante, so I wouldn't be tempted to fall for him, but I did anyway. A lot of times I'd knock on his door in the middle of the afternoon and ask him over for a coke. He always came. He was sweet. Real shy. Mainly he listened to me talk, but when he talked it was about how he was going to be a famous writer someday. And I believed him. I wouldn't be surprised if he is a famous writer. I don't read that much except the newspaper and magazines. You sure you've never heard of him, Joe?" I don't remember her boyfriend's name, but Joe will do.

"Never heard of him," Joe said defiantly. "What's this about him maybe being your boy's father?" he demanded.

That was exactly what I wanted to know.

"It's just that I guess I could see it in his eyes and the way he talked to me, his love for me," Rita said, and I was surprised by the change that had come over her face. She looked years younger. "When my husband left me, I told Mr. Fante about it, and there was such a look of happiness on his face, but I didn't think about it until afterwards because I was real depressed and angry that my husband left me instead of the other way around. It blinded me to everything I had thought and felt and knew was right for me. I had my father help me move back home, and when I told Mr. Fante I was leaving, he practically cried. But I was too angry—my pride was what it was—to see what I had known all along, how he and I were right for each other. It took me a few months to come to my senses. One morning I woke up, and it was real clear; I had to go see Mr. Fante. On the way there I imagined how we'd fall into each other's arms, and the tears would pour, and we'd say how much we loved each other. But when I knocked at the door, an old man answered. He was hard of hearing and it took a while to get him to understand who it was I was looking for. Finally he said, 'Oh, you're looking for a Mr. Fante. I don't know who he is. I'm new here. Come to think of it, I've gotten some mail with a funny name. Maybe that was him.' And then he closed the door. I wrote Mr. Fante a letter to the Bunker Hill address, but I never heard from him. I bet that old man was throwing his mail away."

That's how Mr. Fante could have been my father?

I could see Joe's face in the rearview mirror. It looked dark and gloomy like a coming storm. Rita grew quiet, and Joe didn't say anything. I certainly didn't have anything to say. We rode back home in an eerie silence, and all the way back I kept hoping we'd get in an accident so I'd get killed and wouldn't have to face the kids in the neighborhood. They knew what a dope I was, and now I knew it too.

2

The first map I saw of Los Angeles was a bird's-eye view from the ocean all the way to the desert. My eyes first fell on the countless waves of the Pacific Ocean ceaselessly washing ashore from Malibu to Long Beach and, towering in the distance, the mountains of the Angeles National Forest. Mounts Wilson and Baldy were prominently in view, and beyond the mountains was the Mojave Desert where the habitable world stopped.

I was surprised to find San Pedro on the map. When Rita told me that Uncle Necio had moved to San Pedro, I imagined he had moved somewhere near San Francisco. The only reason I thought he had moved to San Francisco was because of the "San" in San Pedro. I fretted that I might not see him again except for family functions like weddings and funerals. But I soon realized there was nothing to worry about. We continued to see him almost as frequently as we did before he moved. It secretly pleased me to think he thought so much of us that he was continually on the road just to see us. I didn't realize until I saw the map that he had only moved to the other side of Los Angeles, but at first I refused to believe it was the same San Pedro. And so the next time he visited, I grabbed his hand as he came through the door and pulled him to the kitchen table where I had laid out the map.

"What's this about?" Uncle Necio grinned at Rita. She had been telling me for the past half hour to get the map off the table so she could set it for dinner. But I pleaded with her to leave it there until Uncle Necio had a chance to see it.

"I don't know," Rita said shaking her head in a feigned show of disapproval. "I don't know how many times I've told him to get that map off the table, but he keeps insisting that you have to see it first."

My uncle bent his head and gravely inspected the map. He looked at it for what seemed a long time. Then he raised his head and looked at me.

"A map of Los Angeles, huh? What's this? You're studying for a school assignment?"

It was difficult for me to ask him, but it had to be asked.

"Where is San Pedro?"

He grinned, bent his head again and solemnly lowered a thumb on the wrong San Pedro. Then he lifted his thumb. "There," he said as if he had made something and was proudly showing it off. "What, what's the matter?" he said noticing how crestfallen I was.

"It's nothing," I said yanking the map off the table and running to my room. I didn't want him to see my tears.

I didn't leave my room until Rita called me to come and eat. The whole time I was in my room I stared at the map that I had spread out on the bed. Blear-eyed I looked at names like El Segundo and Whittier and Pasadena. I looked at San Fernando and Compton and Glendale. And finally I looked at San Pedro. It shouldn't have bothered me that he had only moved to the other side of Los Angeles and not near San Francisco. It shouldn't have bothered me but it did.

When I went to the table, my uncle had a spoon full of peas he was about to put in his mouth, but when he saw me he lowered the peas back on the plate next to the mashed potatoes.

"Why did you run off like that?" Rita said, a mixture of concern and anger in her voice. I sat in my chair, lowered my head and said a quick prayer, and when I raised my head I noticed the questioning looks of Rita and Uncle Necio.

"Your mother asked you something," my uncle said, trying to sound stern. He sometimes tried to act like my father but fortunately not too often. More often he was like a big brother or a good friend.

"I guess I was disappointed," I said as I lifted up a fork and poked at some peas.

My uncle and Rita exchanged glances.

"Disappointed? What does a little squirt like you have to be disappointed about?" That was Rita, but it could as easily have been my uncle. They both had similar ways of expressing themselves. He was a few years older than her, but I had heard Rita tell someone once that they had been very close growing up, almost as close as twins. It wasn't only apparent in their speech but also in their mannerisms. They had similar ways of winking, a quick wink that if you didn't know them might have seemed like a twitch. They had similar ways of talking to someone. First they had to touch that person, even if it was only a light tap on the elbow or to brush a finger across a person's shirt or blouse. And when they were around me they had a similar playfulness. They loved making up names for me, "Squirt," "Peanut," "Monkey," "Monster," "Midget," "Mr. Serious," and countless other names, many of which they never used more than once or twice because oftentimes they made up the name at the spur of the moment, and after they thought about it, the name didn't make much sense. They both loved the impromptu, which sometimes made them say silly things, but often they made me laugh or at least smile. Of all the names Rita and Uncle Necio called me, I thought the most appropriate was "Mr. Serious." I *was* serious. I couldn't help it. It was how I was.

I noticed Rita and my uncle weren't going to eat until I answered them.

"I thought you had moved further away is all," I said mashing the peas with the fork.

"Is that all it is?" Rita said, and with the same breath, "Stop playing with your food."

"What a funny kid you are," my uncle laughed. "Why don't you two come for a weekend?" Uncle Necio said turning towards Rita. He had asked her several times before, but every time she made some excuse.

"One of these weekends," she said taking a knife and fork and cutting her meat.

"I know you don't like her," my uncle said. "That's no reason—"

"Not in front of him." Rita pointed towards me with her knife.

I hadn't eaten anything yet. I was following their conversation. Before, when Rita had made excuses about not being able to visit my uncle, or avoided the subject, I had thought it was because he lived too far away. But now that I knew he wasn't all that far away, I became very curious. Especially when he brought up someone else, a person I had never met who Rita didn't like.

After Rita pointed at me with her knife, conversation turned towards more typical topics. Rita's complaints about neighbors and her latest boyfriend who had turned out to be a great disappointment and who would have made a terrible father for me. It was a story I had heard for years. And likewise my uncle's latest plans for a new career. He was continually changing jobs.

When my uncle left that night, I helped Rita dry the dishes, and I asked her why she didn't want to visit Uncle Necio in San Pedro.

She looked at me suspiciously as if I had asked her a trick question.

"One of these days we'll go visit your uncle," she said and left it at that.

I went to bed early that night and thought about my Uncle Necio and San Pedro. It came to me that what I was upset about was my ignorance. How stupid to think he had moved near San Francisco.

I felt my face turning red many times as I relived my humiliation. But there was no reason to feel such humiliation. My uncle and Rita hadn't made fun of me. They hadn't thought less of me because of my misunderstanding. But it irked me. It made me realize that the world beyond West Los Angeles was a complete mystery to me. It was both wonderful to think about and also disconcerting. It made me feel insignificant thinking how little I knew about the world.

It was a long night. I had nightmares about San Pedro. When I'd wake up I'd be trembling; I'd only vaguely remember that I had dreamt about going to San Pedro to visit my uncle. But always some terrible thing would happen along the way to prevent me from reaching San Pedro. And always I'd catch a glance of a sinister looking woman. A woman I had never seen before but who I somehow knew was behind all the terrible things that were keeping me from reaching my uncle Necio.

3

I remember the first woman I fell in love with. She had blond curly hair that was cut short about halfway down the back of her neck. She wore a Mexican blouse with ruffles and a red ribbon on the front tied into a bow. The blouse was pulled low revealing handsome shoulders and a goodly portion of her ample breasts. She was sitting down and held a large tray filled to almost overflowing with delicious looking California oranges. She wore an orange colored sombrero, and it was like a halo. She seemed to be holding out her huge tray of oranges for me. Her seductive smile seemed to promise more than just oranges.

Her face looked red from having been out in the sun too long. Her eyes were bedroom eyes, and behind her was everything Los Angeles had to offer: buildings sprouting almost like weeds, oil derricks, the round trees of the orange orchards, thousands of new people arriving each month, the palm trees silhouetted against the sky, the mountains in the background a rosy glow from the setting sun, and snow on the mountain tops. I wasn't even ten. I found her on a label on an old orange crate Rita had brought home to use for something or other but then she changed her mind and gave it to me to keep my comic books in.

I called her Los Angeles. I tried to imagine romances between her and me, but I was too young to understand what that meant. All I knew was everything about her made me desire her, but desire her for what I didn't know. Company, yes. When I read my comic books I would imagine that she was there on the bed with me, and we'd exchange comic books as we'd finish them.

Sometimes we'd just talk, and it'd be hard for me not to stare at her low-cut blouse and what it revealed. If she'd catch me staring at her breasts, I'd pretend I was looking at the oranges on her tray. She never went anywhere without her tray of oranges and her big bright sombrero.

"They look like juicy oranges," I'd say. And then I'd notice her looking down at her breasts. She'd burst out laughing.

"Would you like one?" she'd say, and she'd burst out laughing again seeing me turn so red.

And then she'd say, "Too bad you're so young."

And I'd say, "I don't like being young. Not at all. I'd like to have a job, and a car, and my own house—"

"And a wife?" she'd interrupt, her bedroom eyes penetrating me.

Hard as it was for me to say it, I'd say, "Yes, a wife."

"And of course children," she'd say shifting the weight of the tray, which must have been very tiring because I never saw it leave her lap.

Again I'd turn red. I wasn't exactly clear about how children came about though I knew it had something to do with the relationship between a man and a woman. It had something to do with bedroom eyes and moist lips, which her lips were. It had something to do with undressing, and her blouse was so far down

11

that for me it was almost like being undressed. I wondered if we were having the relationship that caused children. I was experiencing a feeling so unlike anything I had ever felt. I felt flushed and as hot as if I had been standing out in the summer sun all day. And I felt the same giddiness that standing out in the sun all day would have made me feel. I wanted so much to remove the tray of oranges from her lap, but once that happened I didn't know what else would happen. I was hoping that being older, she would take the lead. But then I thought, maybe this is the extent of it, looking at each other with caressing eyes and smiling at each other for long periods of time and then children would follow. I hoped not too many all at one time.

When Rita unexpectedly knocked at my bedroom door, I'd look at Los Angeles with terrified eyes. But there was nothing to fear. Los Angeles was already gone. And when Rita entered the room, she'd see all the comic books scattered over the bed, and she'd say, "It looks like you've had company." And my fear would return. How did she know? But of course she didn't know Los Angeles was there. And once she said, "Have you been eating oranges?" which I adamantly denied. "Funny. It sure smells like oranges in here." And then remembering Los Angeles and her tray of oranges, I'd say, "Oh, yes. I had an orange. Danny down the street gave it to me."

Los Angeles was my first love, and it broke my heart when one day she got off my bed where she was halfway through a comic book and stepped into a red airplane that was waiting for her on top of my dresser. It was a small old fashioned airplane that maybe only held ten or so passengers. As she climbed the stairs into the airplane, she stopped and looked back, being careful not to drop any of her oranges, and blew me a kiss. It was the first kiss we had ever exchanged. "My lovely, lovely Los Angeles," I thought, "I'll never see you again." But fortunately I was wrong. When I needed her, she returned in her little red airplane. And we shared tears. And she promised never to leave me again.

4

When Rita was six, her father waited until everyone at the dinner table had served themselves and had stuffed some food in their mouths before he pulled out a brochure from underneath his empty plate and waved it high over his head. Everyone stopped chewing, their mouths full. It was so unnatural for their father to be acting that way, waving a skinny piece of paper in the air, trying to speak but having a hard time getting the words out in his excitement. His face had turned bright red, and he was flailing his arms so much and gasping for air that he could have been choking on his food, but he hadn't touched anything. The family looked at his clean plate, and they all wondered in dumb terror what could be the matter with him. Several of the smaller children including Rita began to cry.

"Charles!" his wife said in a voice both fearful and questioning, her eyes following the movements of the brochure that she was only now seeing for the first time. She must have wondered how he had slipped it underneath the plate without her seeing him do it. What could it possibly mean?

It didn't take long to find out.

"Ca . . . Ca . . . Cal . . . i . . . fornia," he finally managed to say. The children who were crying stopped crying. Rita wiped away her tears and resumed chewing as did everyone else. "California!" he repeated more clearly. The children looked from their father to their mother for an explanation but immediately looked back at their father. Their mother was as perplexed as they were.

"Says here," he said, waving the brochure vigorously, "a thousand chickens and several roosters for free. All you got to do is buy a house in a place called Van Noose." He meant Van Nuys. "And there's an ocean not that far away, and that's free too," he joked.

The tension in the room relaxed. Everyone smiled. They didn't understand the joke, but they smiled to see him smiling.

"This is the first I've heard of this," his wife said, an anxious sound to her voice but a stoic exterior.

And just a few weeks later they crossed the Colorado River into California. From all that their father had been telling them about California, Rita expected that as soon as they crossed into California everything would magically change. Everything would be green and there would be orchards for as far as the eye could see. They would see sights like that but not for many miles to come. When they crossed from desert into more desert, Rita began wailing that she wanted to go back home. But she wasn't to return to New Mexico for more than ten years, and that was just for a quick visit.

There were seven children, one boy, my uncle Necio, and six girls. Rita was the youngest. And my uncle was next to the youngest.

"We're gonna put you young ones to gather them eggs," their father reminded Rita and my uncle every hundred miles or so. "There's nothing like picking up a warm egg that's just been laid," he'd say. "Instant money."

Rita daydreamed about picking up pennies and nickels and dimes instead of eggs. And the pennies and nickels and dimes would be hot. She'd have to blow in her hands to cool them off.

I heard that story so often, about their moving to California, that for a long time I just assumed I had moved with them. I even thought I remembered seeing the Colorado River for the first time and remembered being disappointed it wasn't wider than it was. And I thought I remembered, when I was real young, waking up to the sound of roosters. But I was born in West Hollywood long after my grandfather's chicken farm had failed.

Things started becoming clear to me one day when I told Rita, "Remember how happy Grandfather was when we were driving across Arizona? He kept saying how rich we all were going to be with those eggs. 'Three hundred people moving to Los Angeles each day, and each and every one of those people good and hungry. It' s easy money.' "

"You couldn't remember that," Rita said giving me a funny look, "you weren't even born then. How could you have been? I was only six years old."

I imagined a six-year-old girl with a five- or six-year-old son. It did seem rather peculiar.

"You weren't born until many years later."

Long after the chicken farm. Long after the crowing of roosters would wake up people to another dry and sunny Los Angeles day.

A large and significant part of my life was suddenly shown to have had no basis in reality.

5

"Mr. Fante," Rita said after lifting up her mop, the floors clean, a chore she hated doing and put off until she couldn't tell any longer if there were bugs on the floor or old dried up pieces of lettuce, watermelon seeds, or other little pieces from meals she had cooked during the month. Sticky places on the kitchen floor, little islands of hair on the bathroom floor, such things were distracting and caused her no end of concern; nevertheless, it usually took her at least a month to build up the energy and enthusiasm to attack the floors. I have to admit, I was just as guilty. I was young, but I could have tried to clean the floors. The most I ever did, though, was sweep them a little. But that was seldom. I shared Rita's concern and anxiety over the floors. It bothered me too that I kept confusing the oval shaped black thing along the wall by the refrigerator for a bug and had stepped on it several times only to realize it was just a watermelon seed. It would have been simple enough to pick it up and throw it in the garbage, but I wouldn't, just like Rita wouldn't, even though I had seen her step on it a few times.

"Mr. Fante," she repeated, looking at me with a clean smile on her face, a smile like an immaculately clean kitchen floor. It made me feel good to see her smile, and the clean kitchen and bathroom floors were something I looked forward to like a special treat. As far as the carpeting in the rest of the house, she didn't have any problem. It was once a week. But the kitchen and bathroom floors, even though they didn't take that long to sweep and mop once she got started, always seemed like a major undertaking. She had to psych herself for days before she did it. And then there was such a glow on her face after she finished. It was like the glow after leaving confession. She gave the floor a final swipe, then lifted the mop. The world was fresh and new.

She put the mop outside to dry.

"Mr. Fante," she said for the third time as she came back into the house. "Whenever I mop the floors, I think of Mr. Fante."

"Why's that?"

"Because he hated to mop his floors too. He liked his floors to be clean, but like me he'd think and think about it, and meanwhile the floors would turn into a real mess. You think I'm bad. You should have seen Mr. Fante's apartment. Everything was neat that was above the floor. He didn't leave clothes just lying around. He always hung them up. He made his bed as soon as he got up, even though he almost never had visitors. I used to tell him, if I wasn't married and didn't have people visiting me, I'd never make the bed. But Mr. Fante said it was how he was brought up. It was more deeply ingrained in him than his Catholicism. He could stay away from church, but he couldn't leave the bed unmade for more than an hour. He always washed his dishes and pans right after he used them. His desk where he had his typewriter, paper, pencils, and dictionary was always orderly with little neat stacks of folders. And each folder had a name for a story he was working on. Everything was perfectly neat until you looked at the floors. Those were linoleum floors. And there'd be old spots of spaghetti sauce on the floor, old wine stains, little shriveled up pieces of vegetables and cheese, and who knows what else. We used to have fun sitting at his table sipping some wine, he always drank wine, and trying to guess what some black, shriveled up thing on the floor was. And sometimes he'd pick it up and bring it up to the table for a closer look. I hated when he did that. I used to mop my floors regularly because my husband expected me to, but I empathized with Mr. Fante. I was just like him. And with time I was less regular about cleaning the floors. It was only one of many ways my husband and I were seeing different. And then one day he didn't come home and that was it. And as far as I was concerned it was good riddance.

"After my husband left, my floors got dirtier and dirtier. And they came to resemble Mr. Fante's floors. But eventually Mr. Fante's dirty floors got to be too much even for him, and one day he gave them a good cleaning. When I went over to tell him my husband had left me, I momentarily forgot all about it when I saw how clean his floors were. 'Mr. Fante, what have you done?' I said, and I'm sure it must have sounded like a shriek. He was sitting at the kitchen table with a large glass of red wine in front of him, and he was staring at the floor as if he couldn't figure out how such a clean floor happened to be in his apartment. He shrugged his shoulders as if to say it was a momentary lapse. But I understood. I understood he hated dirty floors as much as I did. But like with me, it was something he'd rather put off than do.

" 'Now that my husband's left me, I'm gonna see how dirty my floors can get.'

"That's how I told him my husband left me. But already my floors were about as dirty as any floors should get. Mr. Fante had a look on his face like he was about to cry, and a few small tears did roll down. We embraced, and he held me real tight. When he let go, he looked at me funny, and for some reason I thought he was going to propose. But he was such a shy man, he didn't say anything. And then I thought, this is crazy; he wouldn't want to marry me. He let go of me to pour me a glass of wine, but I told him I had to go. Lots to do and think about. I should have stayed. I think he would have built up his nerve to propose. He was so shy. A few times, before I moved out, it seemed to me like he was trying to bring something up. But he'd stumble over his words and then he'd change the subject, his face lobster red. If I hadn't been so young and distracted by my husband leaving me, even though I was glad about it, I might have seen what Mr. Fante was feeling. But I was too young. Only seventeen. I didn't see how much he loved me until I thought about it months later. I couldn't afford to stay in Bunker Hill by myself, so I moved back in with my parents until I got a job. I never saw Mr. Fante again.

"Mr. Fante," she said for the final time, a girlish look to her face. A look of contentment and being at peace with the world.

6

Rita always treated me like a grown-up. So did my uncle Necio.
Before he moved to San Pedro, he lived in Venice. He lived on
the top floor of a white house that was divided into four
apartments. It actually looked like two identical houses joined
in the middle by an enclosed staircase that led to the top two
apartments. Outside his door was a wooden balcony where he
hung his swimming trunks and towels when he came back from
the beach. I didn't understand why he went to the beach when
there was such a wonderful canal just across the sidewalk. But I
never saw anyone swimming there except ducks, so maybe it
wasn't allowed. My greatest pleasure was to float on the canal
in Uncle Necio's rowboat. There were tiny docks along the canal
where we tied up the boat when we wanted to float in the same
place. It was marvelous. It upset me deeply when I learned he
had moved: no more floating peacefully in the rowboat, no more
feeding the ducks, no more sitting with Uncle Necio on his balcony looking at the gently flowing water of the canal while the
sun set and the oppressive heat of the day began to lessen.

Uncle Necio was a college graduate and always had a good
paying job. But he couldn't put up with the same job for more
than two or three years. He claimed that once a job became routine, he had to go. The same thing happened with Rita. She
was always changing jobs, and though we moved a lot, we
mainly stayed in the West Hollywood area.

Rita only went up to the tenth grade, but she was as smart as
my uncle Necio. He tried to discourage her from changing jobs so
often because without a diploma she would find herself having
to start at the bottom all over again. But Rita's jobs were seldom challenging, so they became routine very quickly, and
boredom set in. Also, friction was inevitable between her and
one or more of her co-workers. Her job changes were yearly. If
not for my uncle, we would have often gone hungry. He always
helped us out with money, did repairs around the house, and
he'd take us out places. When we were together, we were all
three equals. But when he'd bring a date, or Rita would bring a
date, things changed. Their dates inevitably gave me funny

looks as if I talked too much, which I resented because I never talked half as much as they did. I'd sometimes hear them say things like, "He's sure precocious," or, "Are you sure he's not a midget instead of a kid?" It hurt me.

I loved it when Rita and Uncle Necio threw new words at me. They encouraged me to use them even though I didn't always know what they meant. They took the time to correct me when I made mistakes. But their dates looked at me as if I was the biggest idiot who had ever lived. I think they resented that my vocabulary was bigger than theirs. Fortunately Rita and Uncle Necio changed relationships more often than they changed jobs, especially Rita. The only thing constant in their lives was their friendship. And me.

At times I'd remind my uncle about the canal along his old apartment in Venice.

"It was a great place," he'd agree.

And then I'd say, "Why did you have to move, then? It was great with the ducks and the rowboat that had been white, and I helped you paint it blue because that's my favorite color."

Uncle Necio would forlornly shake his head remembering those good times.

"It was a bad move."

"It sure was," Rita couldn't help piping in when she caught drift of that conversation.

At that time I didn't know the story behind my uncle's move to San Pedro, but I knew it had something to do with a woman Rita hated. And as long as he lived with her, visiting him was out of the question. But fortunately he continued to drop by though not nearly as often as when he had lived in Venice. I suspected Rita was jealous of that woman. She and my uncle had been so close for so long. But I couldn't see just jealousy being behind that. That woman must have done something terrible to make Rita hate her so much is what I thought.

Even though Rita only went to the tenth grade, she read all the time. I thought I had the smartest mother ever. She'd always try out new words on me that she'd come across in her reading, and so my vocabulary mushroomed way beyond what was normal for my age. I'd try out my new words on my uncle, and sometimes he'd straighten me out on a word or two, but usually I'd get the words right. Rita and Uncle Necio were never defensive. Not like other grown-ups.

I loved the way Uncle Necio would hold his fingers and bring them up to his lips as if he held a cigar. Thumb underneath and fingers laid out like falling dominoes: a couple fingers along the ridge of the imaginary cigar and the other fingers trailing away. He'd take a slow careful draw, his eyebrows crinkled above his nose, registering the inner peace this moment of relaxation brought him.

He had smoked for two years until one day he realized that he relished the thought of smoking more than the actual physical act—it only left him feeling nauseated. This realization occurred while watching a Marx Brothers movie he had taken us to see. When we left the movie theater, he turned to me and said, "Watch." And he lifted his fingers up to his mouth, thumb underneath, two fingers above perfectly positioned to handle a cigar, and the other two fingers trailing off. It was a perfect imitation of how Groucho Marx had held his cigar in the movie, and my uncle's demeanor became very much like Groucho's.

"What are you doing?" Rita said, as we stood on the sidewalk outside the movie theater. It had been a Saturday matinee, so it was still bright out.

"What does it look like I'm doing?" Uncle Necio said, talking through a corner of his mouth, the imaginary cigar dangling from the other corner of his mouth, his eyebrows moving up and down like Groucho had done in the movie.

"I don't know," Rita grimaced. "You're acting stupid it seems to me."

"It's Groucho!" I almost yelled. My uncle moved his eyebrows up and down with great vigor and pretended to take several puffs from his invisible cigar.

"Really," Rita said in mock disapproval, "I think Michael acts more grown-up than you."

I stared at Rita, surprised to hear her say my name. Usually she'd use nicknames like "Mr. Serious" or "Pasadena." I liked the name Pasadena. The name came about after we visited a small amusement park there. I had so much fun at the amusement park that every chance I got I pestered Rita and Uncle

Necio to take me back. Finally one night Rita yelled, "Shut up with Pasadena!" It shut me right up. I shut up because of the tone of her voice, but Rita must have thought it was the word Pasadena that put me in my place. So anytime she wanted me to behave, she'd say "Pasadena" in as stern a voice as she could muster. And I'd behave, partly because of the tone of her voice and partly because her saying the word Pasadena gave me hope we'd go back there. But for some reason we never did even though Uncle Necio often hinted we would.

"Groucho!" I insisted to Rita as I pointed at my uncle. It was difficult to keep my laughter in check.

"Little Pasadena here knows of what he speaks," my uncle said. "Oh, did I tell you? I shot an ostrich in my pajamas. What it was doing in my pajamas I'll never know."

"An elephant," I corrected my uncle before bursting into giggles.

"Are you implying I'm as fat as an elephant?" Uncle Necio said, pretending to be insulted. That put an immediate stop to my giggling. But then he winked, and I was back to giggling.

"Why did the chicken cross the road?" my uncle asked, still talking through a corner of his mouth and pretending to take an occasional puff. I actually saw a long brown cigar.

Knowing my uncle, I suspected it was a trick question. Who hadn't heard that joke before, but I knew he had a twist to it.

" 'Cause there weren't any cigars on its side of the road," I giggled.

Rita looked around to see if people were listening to us. She never got crazy like we did. It embarrassed her to think people might be listening to us.

"Nope," my uncle said taking the cigar out of his mouth. "She heard a place across the road was paying chicken feed."

I laughed heartily even though I didn't think his joke was all that funny. What I really laughed at was the furious motion of his eyebrows and the way he plopped his nonexistent cigar back in his mouth and puffed away at it furiously. I could really see the smoke.

Rita frowned at us, but I could see she liked seeing us enjoy ourselves.

From then on my uncle stopped smoking. When he got the urge to smoke, he'd do his Groucho Marx imitation. That's when he was around us. I wondered if he did the same thing at work and wondered if people there thought it was as funny as I did. I asked Rita once and she said she thought he locked himself in his office when he did it. Anyway, she hoped he did.

"Maybe that's why he changes jobs so much," I suggested.

"Maybe," Rita said with a wry smile.

After he lost his urge to smoke, Uncle Necio ended his Groucho Marx routine. And no matter how much I hounded him about it, he refused to bring his fingers to his lips with his thumb underneath, carefully cradling the cigar as if it were made of the most fragile material that would shatter if he held it too tight. And his eyebrows. I couldn't get him to wriggle his eyebrows anymore. Sometimes I'd go into the bathroom and lock the door and practice wriggling my eyebrows in the mirror. But it wasn't funny when I did it. It didn't even make me smile.

Oh, yeah, why did the chicken cross the road?

Because a place across the road was paying chicken feed. Only the stupid chicken didn't realize it was a fried chicken place.

I made that one up long after my uncle stopped doing his Groucho Marx imitation. I meant to tell it to him, but I kept forgetting.

7

Santa Monica Beach was my favorite. It was the nearest beach to where we lived, so we always went there. The few times we tried other beaches, Rita agreed with me; Santa Monica was the best. We mainly went there in the winter when there weren't so many people. Rita would say she liked people individually, even two or three at a time could be fine, but more than that she couldn't stand. She meant it on a personal basis, because of course living in Los Angeles made it impossible to avoid crowds. That's why she turned down all invitations to parties, but a baseball game was okay because she didn't know any of the people and didn't have to talk to them. Most crowds she could handle as long as she didn't have to interact. But on the beach, it was different. I guess it was the lack of clothing that made it seem more personal to her. The summer crowds on the beach drove her crazy, but on weekdays in the winter there were few people there. And most of the people would be at a distance from the water sunning themselves. Rita and I could walk along the undulating edge of the water and hardly anyone else would be out walking. The winter skies in Santa Monica were clear. The weather perfect.

Rita always changed jobs during the winter. And she wouldn't take another job until she had to. All year she'd save so there'd be money for the rent and food. And if she couldn't find a job when she went looking, Uncle Necio was always there to help. He wouldn't bat an eye when Rita would tell him she needed three or four hundred. And three and four hundred dollars was worth a lot more then than it is now. Much more. Rita always insisted she'd pay Uncle Necio back. But he'd say, "It's a present. Don't worry." And after a short time, she wouldn't worry. I don't think she ever paid him back even a dollar. He ate at our house often, but usually he brought big bags of groceries with him. She washed his clothes and ironed them, even after he moved to San Pedro to live with that woman Rita hated. Rita would say, "She won't even sew a button on for him much less wash and iron his clothes."

I vaguely knew that the woman Uncle Necio lived with was an artist and made a living from selling her paintings. He almost never mentioned her when Rita was in hearing range, but once when we went alone for hot dogs—Rita hated hot dogs because she said she knew what they were made of—to the Tail o' the Pup, which was only a few blocks away from my house, he confided in me as we waited for the hot dogs. Her name was Angelica, which startled me a little because it reminded me of the name of my first and only true love, Los Angeles. "Don't tell your mother I told you," Uncle Necio made me promise. And then he told me that Angelica was beautiful, but she did things that some people thought were kinda crazy. I knew Rita was one of those people, but I didn't say anything. He said that she had struggled for a long time to get where she was at, and she had paid a price for it. It had required that she be selfish in many ways and strong willed. And often she was opinionated and was good at starting arguments. She was older than him and kept telling him to quit his job because she made enough money for both of them. But he couldn't see that. I agreed. A man should pay his way to keep his self-esteem. We ate the hot dogs leaning against the Tail o' the Pup, which was a small stand shaped like a hotdog bun with the hot dog sticking out at either end. I was so pleased by Uncle Necio taking me into his confidence that I almost spilled the beans about my love affair with Los Angeles. When we got back home I was relieved I hadn't said anything. What would he have thought of me?

And on the way back home the reason Rita hated Angelica came out—or one of the reasons. She had been so busy with her career that she hadn't had any children. And now it was too late, and she regretted it. She had called Rita on the phone and asked—demanded according to Rita—to adopt me. She had never met me or Rita, and she had called without telling Uncle Necio what she intended to do—he always talked about me so she knew me that way and from a photo. She called Rita and said she and Uncle Necio could offer me a much better life, so Uncle Necio should bring me to San Pedro the next time he visited. I remembered how upset Uncle Necio was at the time. Angelica didn't say a word about the phone call. He didn't learn about it until Rita confronted him. Uncle Necio shook his head from side to side as we walked back to the house. I almost cried seeing such sadness in his eyes and the sorrow in his voice. Walking back home from the Tail o' the Pup, there was plenty of time to hear as much as he wanted to tell me. A block from the house Uncle Necio stopped and looked at me. "Remember. What I said is confidential. I love your mother as much as any brother could love his sister. And I love you as if you were my son. It hurts me that you can't get to know Angelica and that she can't come to visit. I know she and your mother would come to love each other if they gave each other a chance. Then you could visit us in San Pedro, and I could take you to see the ships that dock there. It's such a shame how things have worked out. But that's how it is. Your mother and Angelica are too strong willed to have it any other way. You put them together and there'd be an explosion." I thought my uncle was going to cry. His voice sounded as if he were talking about someone he loved who had died. "Remember what I said. This is just between us."

Walking that last block to the house, I almost blurted out my secret love for Los Angeles. Los Angeles with her short curly blond hair and her friendly outgoing nature. I knew she and Uncle Necio would hit it off. But finally I didn't tell him not just because she was an image on a paper label but because I feared they'd fall in love. When we got to the house I quickly rushed to my room and turned the crate so the label couldn't be seen. Uncle Necio sometimes came into my room, but luckily he had never seen Los Angeles, and as far as I could tell, she hadn't noticed him either. I turned the crate just in time.

"Why in such a hurry?" Rita said entering the room with Uncle Necio right behind her.

Uncle Necio had a worried look as if I might reveal everything he had confided to me.

"I wanted to see if my comic books were still here." That was the best I could come up with at the spur of the moment.

"Of course they would still be here." Rita gave Uncle Necio a questioning look.

"Children always worry that their mothers are going to throw their comic books away," Uncle Necio said in my defense. I was impressed. I could never think that fast.

"It's the hot dogs," Rita said turning around and walking out of the room with Uncle Necio right behind her. "I told you not to take him for hot dogs. Remember I worked in that meat packing plant? Didn't I tell you what they put in them?"

I sat at the edge of my bed and thought of Angelica and Rita and Uncle Necio and Los Angeles, Los Angeles my love and Los Angeles the city. They're all stars in the movie of my life, I thought. And I hoped the ending would be a good one. And then I thought about Rita not liking to be around too many people. Why didn't she leave Los Angeles if she felt that way? I knew she was a woman with a tremendous ability to love. I felt that love in profound ways. So did my uncle Necio. I think that's why he spent so much time with us. I remembered going to Santa Monica Beach with Rita and how she'd call the school and tell them I was sick and would be out for two or three days. We'd walk along the beach barefooted. She would shy away from the waves, but I'd let them splash me even though they were cold. And she would let me walk through the water as long as I didn't get in much deeper than my ankles. Thinking back, I realize Rita would have been an extremely lonely person if she hadn't had me and Uncle Necio in her life.

8

When Angelica and Uncle Necio broke up after almost a year of living together, Rita was triumphant. Uncle Necio arrived at our door drunk one night. He had a key so he let himself in and fell asleep on the couch. Rita and I had been asleep for hours. I didn't even know he was there until I went to the kitchen to have breakfast. Rita whispered to me to be quiet. From the kitchen counter where I often had my cereal and milk, I could see Uncle Necio stretched out on the couch. A blanket was over him and he was snoring, but he seemed to be fully clothed.

"Why does Uncle Necio wear his clothes to bed?" I whispered to Rita who hovered over me as I ate and kept casting occasional glances at Uncle Necio.

"He left that woman," she said in the same kind of voice someone might use if they won a million dollars but were being cautious just in case it wasn't true.

And I thought, when you end a relationship it means you can do anything you want. You don't take your clothes off to go to bed, you don't brush your teeth, you don't take a shower or comb your hair. I thought Uncle Necio was lucky, and it seemed to me worthwhile to end a relationship so you could do what you wanted. But I also felt some sadness remembering when Uncle Necio had confided in me about Angelica when we went for hot dogs at the Tail o' the Pup. I remembered she was an artist and had worked so hard at becoming successful that she didn't have time to have children. And now she didn't have Uncle Necio. The look on Rita's face told me it was final between Uncle Necio and Angelica. Uncle Necio groaned and sat up on the couch. He ran his fingers through his hair and looked in my direction. There was a pained expression on his face that I thought was his grief for having left Angelica, but when he got up and rushed to the bathroom and threw up, I realized it was from too much drinking. I had to catch the bus, so I was gone when Uncle Necio came out of the bathroom. When I got home from school, Rita was there and so was Uncle Necio. They were at the living room table drinking coffee and talking. I was disappointed to see he was wearing different clothes than he had been that morning—he kept clothes at our house—and his hair was neatly combed. What's the use of breaking up, I thought.

Uncle Necio had only talked to me about Angelica that one time at the Tail o' the Pup. He had told me how much he loved her and how sad it made him that Rita and Angelica didn't get along. The pained expression that was on Uncle Necio's face early in the morning was gone. He smiled at me as I came in the house. It was like nothing was different. Except he stayed with us until he found an apartment. I tried to get him to look for a place in Venice where he had lived before moving to San Pedro. I remembered how much fun it was riding in his blue rowboat along the canal. He sometimes would complain that the water had a bad smell, but it didn't bother me. No, he found a place just a few blocks from where we lived. The consolation for me was that it was only a block away from the Tail o' the Pup.

There were many times I wanted to ask him about Angelica, but I was afraid to bring it up. I kept hoping he would confide in me like he had that time at the Tail o' the Pup when he had told me she was a difficult woman but he loved her. And it fascinated me that someone could make a living drawing and painting. And for a while I daydreamed I would visit Angelica with Uncle Necio. He would leave me alone with her while he would go do something. And she would let me do anything I wanted in her studio. By the time Uncle Necio returned, the studio would be a mess with canvases filled with finger painting, spilt paint on the floor, and broken pastels and crayons everywhere. Even paint on the walls. And Uncle Necio would say, "My God, you've made a mess," but Angelica would say, "Necio, Necio, don't discourage the young boy. Don't you see he's talented? He could be a famous artist someday. Little by little I'll teach him. You'll see. He'll be even more famous than me."

But Uncle Necio never confided in me again about Angelica even though we went to the Tail o' the Pup many times despite Rita's protest that hot dogs weren't good for me.

It was strange. It was like a year had passed that was ripped out of our lives. No mention was ever made of Uncle Necio having lived in San Pedro. The only difference was that for a long time Rita was cheerier than usual. Uncle Necio seemed the same. They loved each other, Uncle Necio and Rita. I guess that's why relationships never worked for them. Their friendship was too strong to allow anyone else in their lives for any length of time. Except for me, of course. And Halcy. I'll explain later. And Mr. Fante. If he had knocked at the door and proposed, Rita would have said yes in an instant. But then, I wonder, how could the real Mr. Fante have competed with the memory she had nurtured over so many years.

9

There were times someone would knock at the door, and I would think, what if it's Mr. Fante come to propose to Rita? It never was Mr. Fante, but it never stopped me from imagining what it would be like if he actually came to our door.

Rita opens the door. I'm looking at TV and don't bother to see who it is.

"Oh my God!" Rita exclaims. I turn to look. It's a man I've never seen before. Rita is standing there with a hand over her mouth. She removes her hand and repeats, "Oh my God. After all these years. Can it really be you?" I look at the man again. He looks ordinary. I look back at the TV program I was watching.

"Come in, come in," I hear Rita say. And then the door closes. "Michael, Michael, I want you to meet Mr. Fante."

Fante!? I think. That ordinary looking man is Mr. Fante? I completely forget about the TV program even though it's my favorite sitcom. I stand up and turn around to face Mr. Fante.

He's looking at me intently. He doesn't look quite so ordinary now that I know he's Mr. Fante. In fact, he's beginning to look like one of the most intriguing men I've ever seen. He could be a lion tamer who sticks his head in the mouths of lions. Or he could be a world famous mountain climber who's just returned from climbing the highest mountain in the world for the tenth time.

"Hello, young man," Mr. Fante says. He extends his hand. I walk around the sofa and shake his hand. Some people try to impress you, or intimidate you, by squeezing your hand real hard until it hurts, but Mr. Fante doesn't. Already I see I'm going to like him.

After shaking hands, I say, "I've heard a lot about you, Mr. Fante."

Mr. Fante glances at Rita. "I hope it's all been good?" he says looking back at me.

"Yes, sir, very good." I don't know what else to say.

"Come sit down," Rita says looking flustered. I know she's thinking, why did he have to come by when I look like such a mess? "Turn off that TV, Michael."

Rita pulls a chair from the dining room table and tells Mr. Fante to sit.

"What will you have to drink, Mr. Fante?" Rita says wringing her hands. "Some wine? A beer?"

"You don't have to call me Mr. Fante," Mr. Fante says. "Call me John."

"I don't know if I can. All these years I've been remembering you as Mr. Fante."

"Please try."

Mr. Fante—I can't imagine calling him John—is wearing a light blue pullover shirt, no pocket. His hair is short and combed back with a part almost in the middle. It looks funny to me. I had never really thought much about how he would look, but having stood next to him, I'm disappointed by how short he is. Uncle Necio is several inches taller than him, and I've never thought of Uncle Necio as being a tall man.

"Come and talk with Mr. Fante—I mean John." Rita's face turns red. I had stayed standing by the TV after I turned it off. I take a chair across from Mr. Fante. It wobbles. All the chairs at the table wobble.

"How about a cool glass of wine or beer, Mr. . . . . I mean John?"

"A glass of wine would be just great," Mr. Fante says. He had been smiling affably before, but now there's a haggard look on his face, the kind of look I sometimes see on Rita's face by the end of the week, but this is just Monday.

"Coke on ice for me," I say.

"You know where you can get it," Rita says as she pours Mr. Fante a glass of red wine over ice. She pours herself a glass while I get my coke. I decide to drink it straight out of the bottle.

Mr. Fante watches me take my first drink, which is a long one. I hadn't realized how thirsty I was.

"Doesn't that bring back memories?" Mr. Fante says directing Rita's attention to my coke.

"Sure does," Rita says sitting down and taking a sip from her glass of wine.

"There weren't any better times than those in Bunker Hill," Mr. Fante says.

"It sure was fun drinking cokes," Rita admits, looking at my coke, her voice sounding different than I've ever heard it before, almost like a teenager's voice. I put my coke on the table and lower my eyes. All the attention is making me self-conscious, even if they're only looking at the coke bottle.

"Well, tell me," Rita says, "did you ever get any books published? I've looked in libraries and hundreds of bookstores, but I've never seen any."

Mr. Fante's expression is even more tired looking now. It's the kind of look you'd expect from someone who's weary with life.

"Not much. I had one book published years ago, but the publisher went broke. They were sued by Hitler and the German government, can you believe it? That was around 1939. My publisher published *Mein Kampf* without permission. Can you believe that bastard Hitler got away with suing an American publisher? Anyway, it ruined them. And there went my book."

"I can't believe it," Rita says dismayed. "Hitler?" She pours herself and Mr. Fante another glass of wine. I'm surprised to see her drink so fast. Usually she nurses her drink.

"I've had some other novels published and some stories. But nothing much happens. They get published and that's it. That's why I've been screenwriting. It pays the bills."

I'm impressed. The movies. Maybe I can tell him about my love affair with Los Angeles. I think it would make a terrific movie. How a young boy falls madly in love with a much older woman. A woman who is extremely attractive and represents all the best attributes of the city of Los Angeles. I think of rushing into my room and bringing out my orange crate with sweet, dear Los Angeles on the label. Los Angeles with her winning smile, her perfect teeth, her short, curly golden hair. But then I realize it would be too soon to bring up Los Angeles. Maybe if we get to know each other better. But I'm glad to know I have a connection to Hollywood. Los Angeles will be impressed when I tell her.

"Really?" Rita says. I've never seen her so mesmerized by anyone. He could have told her he had been elected president of the United States, and she wouldn't have been any more impressed. And then she notices his wedding ring for the first time. It's not the sort of thing I would have noticed if I didn't see her staring at it. There's such a shocked look on her face.

"You noticed the ring. I *am* married, but we decided to get a divorce. I don't know why we ever got married. We never agree on anything." Rita's face turned pale. "I'm here to ask you if you'll marry me as soon as the divorce is final." Mr. Fante takes off his wedding ring and puts it in his pocket. The blood returns to Rita's face. "I've been wearing the ring so long, I didn't think about it. You know, a habit."

From despair to joy, Rita's face has regained the look it had when she introduced me to Mr. Fante.

"I've thought about you so much all these years," Rita says. "Didn't you ever get that letter I sent you to your Bunker Hill address?"

"Letter? No, I never got a letter. You mean there was a letter?"

"I knew it. That old man who moved into your apartment threw it in the garbage. What a horrible man."

"What did the letter say?"

"It said I hoped we'd still be able to keep seeing each other."

"Damn, and I thought you didn't care about me. I thought, what would such a beautiful young woman want with me? Our lives could have been so different."

"The years wasted," Rita says, looking at me, and I wonder if I'm part of the wasted years she's referring to. Has to be. There haven't been many other years than those. Fortunately she says, "If not for Michael, it would have been impossible."

"He's a great looking boy," Mr. Fante says. I feel very embarrassed and try not to look at them. But I'm feeling pleased they think so highly of me.

"So, do you want to marry me?"

"And Michael?"

"You, Michael, we'll make a great family."

"Of course I'll marry you. You're the only man I've ever really loved." Rita jumps up and embraces him. But then she lets go of him when he doesn't return the embrace. She waits for him to kiss her. But he doesn't. A shadow crosses Rita's face as she nervously refills their wine glasses. I suddenly notice the tension in the air. I was going to ask for a second coke thinking it's time to celebrate. But seeing the tears on Rita's face, I realize the time to ask has passed. I turn to look at Mr. Fante to try to find an explanation for his strange behavior. Mr. Fante's face has vanished. The rest of his body is there, but above his neck nothing. I begin to cry.

But I could never imagine anything more than that. Mr. Fante at the door. Rita answering. A conversation at the dining room table. The proposal. Rita's acceptance. And then the horrible disappearance of Mr. Fante's head. Head or no head, it was a great disappointment to me that Mr. Fante never knocked at the door. And I imagine it was a great disappointment to Rita as well.

10

I remember learning the names of the mountains around Los Angeles. They were like magical incantations: the Santa Monicas, the Tehachapis, the San Gabriels, the San Bernardinos, and the Santa Anas. It was an assignment the teacher had given the class, but I didn't know about it until five minutes before school started on Friday morning. Even though I had missed the rest of the week, I was the third student the teacher called on to recite the names. The teacher didn't like me much and didn't hesitate at the opportunity to humiliate me in front of the class.

Early Monday morning Rita had phoned in to say I was sick, but I'm sure no one was fooled when I returned to school with a tan. We had a great time taking a leisurely drive to Monterey, stopping often to explore the beaches and fill paper bags with interesting rocks, shells, and driftwood. Or when it was too steep to get down to the beach, we sat for long periods perilously close to the edges of cliffs and just enjoyed the scenery. It was what Rita called meditating, being quiet and relaxing. After a while I'd feel like I was part of the sky, part of the water, part of the mountains. I was greatly disappointed when Rita said I had to go back to school on Friday. It didn't make much sense to me to go back for just one day, but then she explained that in a couple weeks she'd take me out for a whole week, and, besides, she had to be back in Los Angeles on Friday to fill out some papers to cash in her retirement from the job she had just quit. Most of her jobs didn't have retirement plans, and for that reason Uncle Necio had tried to talk her out of quitting. But he should've known better. Rita needed two or three months off each year, and no employer was going to give her that much time off. Besides, it didn't take her long to get tired of the people she worked with.

Anyway, to get back to the names of the mountains around Los Angeles. If I had been in school on Thursday, it would have been easy enough to memorize the five names that night, but as it was, I only learned about the assignment five minutes before class started because a girl who liked me passed me a list of the names written in pencil in her neat handwriting. I only managed to read through the list a few times before the teacher came in the room and announced for everyone to clear their desks. Even though I was born in Los Angeles, I had never paid attention to the names of the mountains.

The teacher immediately noticed me—and no doubt my tan—but she didn't say anything until she came to my name on the roll call.

"Michael," she said sharply, "I tried to call your mother at night to find out how you were doing. I called two different nights and there was no answer. I was real worried, Michael. I thought maybe you were in the hospital." The teacher didn't look like she had been worried. Her expression and the sound of her voice said she knew or at least suspected what Rita and I were up to. "I had the principal call your mother at work, and they said she had called in early on Monday morning and quit. They had been trying to call her all week and couldn't reach her either."

I had told Rita it was a mistake for me to go to school on Friday, and there was the proof. Feeling panicky, I wondered if I should confess everything, but then I thought that could get Rita in trouble, not to mention the trouble I would be in. I decided to remain quiet.

"Where were you, Michael?"

"At home," I barely managed to say.

"You didn't answer the phone because you were sick?"

"Yes." I was wondering how she was going to try to trick me to spill the beans.

"How about your mother? Where was your mother?"

"At home." I was wondering how Rita would be able to get me out of school in a couple of weeks. She wanted to take me to the zoo in San Diego and then to go visit her friend Halcy in Yuma. They had worked at the same place and that's how they came to know each other. Halcy was the closest thing to a best friend Rita ever had, other than Uncle Necio. I liked Halcy a lot, and I cried when I learned she was moving. I had known her since I was about four, and she had babysat me many times. Rita cried too. Halcy said she was sick and tired of being single. She met men, but none of them ever wanted to marry her. She decided to move to Yuma when she read a magazine article that said small towns abounded with men dying to get married. She chose Yuma because like me she had never been out of California, and she thought she'd have better luck if she moved to another state. But still she hated to leave California, so she settled on Yuma as a compromise. Rita had desperately tried to get Uncle Necio and Halcy together. He was always polite. But when Halcy was not around, he'd tell Rita that Halcy was definitely not his type. He liked women who were educated and had good paying jobs. Halcy was lots of fun, but she hadn't graduated from high school, like Rita, and she just barely managed to pay the bills—again like Rita. In lots of ways she and Rita were so alike. I didn't understand why my uncle didn't see the similarities. He couldn't have; otherwise, I'm sure he would have married Halcy. I always regretted that he didn't. Then she wouldn't have had to move to Yuma. I looked forward to seeing Halcy much more than I did the zoo in San Diego. There was no way I would miss that trip.

"Why didn't your mother answer the phone, Michael?"

All the kids had been deathly quiet. While I thought of something to say, I noticed how unnaturally quiet everyone was. The only other time it had been that quiet was when I had gotten to school early and was the first one in the classroom.

"She was sick," I finally said.

"That's why she didn't answer the phone?"

"Yes." I was afraid that the teacher had heard about the trip Rita and I had taken. I was afraid she'd suddenly call me a liar.

"Could you have your mother call the principal, Michael. We'd like to schedule a meeting with her."

I tried to say I would, but the words stuck in my throat. Finally, I just nodded my head up and down. I was wondering if all the kids knew what a liar I was. I could feel their eyes boring into me.

The teacher continued with her roll call and then immediately began calling on students. After two kids got up and said the names correctly, she came to me.

"I can't have you make up this exam, Michael. If you want to get up and try, it's up to you. Otherwise, I have to give you an 'F.' You really do miss too many classes."

I stood up, my legs trembling.

"Santa Monicas." That one was easy. I couldn't count how many times I had played hooky with Rita at Santa Monica Beach. I thought hard. I knew one started with a 't' and sounded like a place in Mexico my uncle had visited the year before. "Techiapas," I said. Immediately I heard a couple of the other students chuckling.

"The Te-ha-cha-pis," the teacher corrected me. I tried to repeat it, but my tongue came out with something similar to what I had already said. More chuckles.

I thought harder. "Saint Gabriels," I blurted out. This brought a peevish smile from the teacher and laughter from the students.

"Go on," she said sounding as if she didn't really mean it.

The only other name I could think of was Saint Bernards, and I knew that was definitely wrong. I didn't want to give the kids any more reason to laugh than they already had.

"I can't think of any others," I finally said.

"Then sit down," the teacher said. Her words stung me like a paddle.

That Friday was one of the longest days I ever had in school. I kept thinking of the meeting Rita was going to have with the principal and the teacher. I wondered if it would lead to my having to change schools. This was my third school in two years. Rita was always getting into loud arguments with teachers and principals. But I was a studious child, "Mr. Serious," so even with all the days I missed, I always did well enough that I was passed on to the next grade. Rita was always threatening to take me out of school completely and teach me at home. I kept hoping she would, but instead she'd put me in another school. That was one great thing about Los Angeles, plenty of schools nearby.

I took the list of names home, and I went over and over them until it was time to eat. Uncle Necio always ate with us on Friday nights; even when he had lived with that woman in San Pedro, he would still spend Friday nights with us. After we had been eating for a while, I suddenly asked my uncle if he had ever been to the Santa Anas. He said he had driven by them a lot. Then after eating a little longer, I asked him about the San Bernardinos.

"Sure," he said. "They're near the Santa Anas."

Rita gave me a funny look.

"How about the Tehachapis?" I said. I had practiced saying that in my room with the door closed. I was proud I had said it right.

"That's way north," Uncle Necio said, giving me a quizzical look.

"Stop bothering your uncle," Rita said, shaking her head. "Is this what you learned in school today?"

That reminded me of what the teacher had told me to tell Rita.

"The teacher said to call the principal. They want to have a meeting with you."

I was staring at my plate of red chile and meat. When I looked up at Rita, I saw the same fiery red on her face.

"Those . . ." she started but stopped.

"Be careful," Uncle Necio said. "You don't want to have to move him to another school."

We finished eating without anyone saying anything. A couple of times I glanced at Rita to see if her face was still red, which it was. The air was taut with her anger. After eating I excused myself and went to my room. Usually I helped Rita dry the dishes. But she didn't say anything one way or the other when I asked her, so I assumed it was alright to go to my room. When I closed the door of my room, I heard Uncle Necio say something, and then Rita said something in a much louder voice. Then it was quiet for a while. And then they started a conversation, but I could barely hear them, so they must have moved to the living room.

I had been sitting at the edge of my bed for a while before I noticed Los Angeles staring at me out of the side of the orange crate. She had been alone almost all week.

"Michael," she said, "why are you ignoring me?"

I looked at her, and I was startled by how beautiful she was. It was the kind of beauty that had to be seen to be believed. When I thought of her, I could never remember even a fraction of her beauty. So every time I saw her, it was as if I saw her for the first time. And for a moment it was blinding like looking at the sun. When my eyes adjusted to her incredible beauty, I once more found myself falling deeply and hopelessly in love. I thought again for the hundredth time that I had to peel her off the orange crate so I would have her with me always. I would have her laminated and wear her around my neck from a cotton thread. I could even take baths with her without her disintegrating.

"Don't be like this, Michael. Don't shun me. How have I offended you?"

"No, no, my sweet Los Angeles. You could never do anything to offend me. Please forgive me, my love, my life, my darling Los Angeles, but it's been a rough day."

"Would you like an orange?"

Los Angeles offered me her tray of oranges that she always had handy.

I shook my head and said, "I just ate but thank you."

I started taking off my clothes to go to bed, but for the first time I felt self-conscious having Los Angeles watch me undress. I turned the crate so she couldn't see me. But once in bed I got lonely for Los Angeles, so just wearing my shorts, I got out of bed and turned the crate so Los Angeles and I could see each other.

Los Angeles was crying.

"The Santa Monicas, the Tehachapis, the San Gabriels, the San Bernardinos, the Santa Anas . . . " I said it over and over not knowing what else to say to comfort her. Each time I said it, it sounded more like a magical incantation. By the fifth or sixth time of saying the names, I noticed a change in Los Angeles's expression. The tears dried up and she began to smile.

"You're so funny, Michael," she finally said. "You can make me smile no matter what. I love you, Michael, more than any label on an old orange crate could ever love anyone. Have I ever complained about you filling up my crate with comic books? I hate comic books, but for you I tolerate them. Oh, Michael, you are my whole life."

"I love you," I whispered. And then I told Los Angeles about my plans of someday laminating her so I could wear her around my neck, and she could go everywhere with me.

"Do it, Michael," she pleaded. "Do it soon."

I promised her I would. But I never did, and I know that must have broken her heart. She never brought it up, but until the day Rita threw her and the comic books away, I felt a hurt and sadness coming from her that had never been there before.

I fell asleep thinking of the names of the mountains around Los Angeles, saying them over and over in my head like an incantation. They became living things, like animals, but animals I had never seen before, or not exactly. The San Gabriels were like a mixture of a rhinoceros and some flying prehistoric animal whose name I couldn't recall. The Santa Anas were like salamanders but with hooves and a dog's tail. The San Bernardinos were like dying mastodons but with fish tails and pigs' feet. The Santa Monicas were part dwarf, like a dwarf out of a fairy tale, but with udders like a cow and a long alligator's tail. And the Tehachapis were like bounding African animals, not antelope, but something like them, except they had orangutan faces and a tail with barbs. Surprisingly, I didn't have any nightmares that night.

11

How I loved my sweet Los Angeles. Curly blond hair and eternal smile. My first and greatest love.

I went into shock when I found her missing. Her, the orange crate she was attached to, and the comic books that were in the orange crate.

I was in tears when I rushed into the kitchen where Rita was peeling potatoes. There was a guilty look on her face, but she kept peeling the potatoes and staring straight into the sink.

"Where . . . where's Los Angeles?" I blurted out, hot tears burning their trails down my cheeks. Rita, a blurry figure.

Rita put a peeled potato in a blue bowl next to the sink. She placed the knife on the counter. She turned slowly to look at me.

"Los Angeles? What are you talking about, Michael?"

"The orange crate with the comic books. Los Angeles is on the orange crate. What did you do with her?" I was blubbering like a five-year-old child.

"If you mean the comic books, Michael, I've been telling you for a long time that you waste too much time with them. I threw them in the trash." I looked in the direction of the door.

"They're gone, Michael. The trash was picked up this morning."

I ran back to my room and locked the door behind me. Rita knocked softly at the door. I stared at the empty place where Los Angeles had sat for the past two years. I had spent countless hours staring at her and the dark silhouettes of palm trees to either side of her. Behind her the story of Los Angeles, the city, unfolded: orange orchards, oil derricks, movie stars arriving in beautiful red airplanes, the city mushrooming to the foothills of the snowcapped mountains. And Los Angeles sitting before it all proudly holding her tray of prize oranges. Los Angeles with her orange colored sombrero, her face and shoulders glowing from having spent another day under a sunny sky without a trace of a cloud.

After knocking a little, Rita left. I fell on the bed and wept. "Why, why, why?" I kept saying over and over. After a while Rita came back to the door and said it was time to eat. I didn't stir, but kept thinking of Los Angeles. What a horrible fate. Buried in trash. Her white satin dress ruined, her trayful of oranges scattered and lost in the garbage. Her orange sombrero crushed. And that radiant smile that I thought was eternal, gone. Her eyes gone dry, her eyelids painfully stiff from continual weeping. The world gone totally dark. Los Angeles, the city, no longer visible to Los Angeles the woman. The woman who gave birth to it all only to end up in its dump under tons of garbage. My eyes grew dry from continually crying, my eyelids became stiff and painful.

In the morning Rita knocked softly at my door. I hadn't slept all night. I must have said "why?" a million times.

"I left you something to eat on the table, Michael," Rita said. "I have to go to work. You have to go to school, Michael," and then she left.

I didn't go to school. Most of the day I stared at the empty place where Los Angeles had been. My love, my sweetheart, my wife to be, she was gone. And there would never be anyone like her again.

12

Uncle Necio insisted that Rita should go see Halcy on her own. He met with my teacher and principal because he was afraid of how Rita would react, and, as he said to Rita, it was too close to the end of the school year to put me in a new school. The day before we were to leave on our trip, I woke up to my uncle and Rita shouting at each other. When I woke up the next morning, I found Uncle Necio at the kitchen table reading a newspaper. This in itself wasn't unusual because Uncle Necio often slept over or sometimes he stopped for breakfast on his way to work. But what was unusual was that Rita wasn't anywhere in sight, and that she had let me sleep late when we were supposed to get an early start on our trip. Seeing me come into the kitchen, Uncle Necio put down his newspaper.

"We're gonna have a great time you and me," he said, and I knew instantly that Rita had left to see Halcy. I was greatly disappointed, but the disappointment didn't last long.

When I got back from school, Uncle Necio was waiting for me to rush me off somewhere fun. Every night was the same, and the weekend was even better. We saw drag racing at the County Fairgrounds in Pomona. At the Riverside Raceway, I decided a Porsche was the kind of car I wanted. We went to Santa Anita and Hollywood Park where Uncle Necio tried to get me to bet on the horses, but instead I held tightly to the two dollars he had given me. I saw how quickly he had lost twenty dollars, and there was no way I was parting with my two dollars. Not on a bet, anyway. That gave Uncle Necio an opportunity to give me a new nickname: "Tight Money." I kinda liked the name. We went to the Movieland Wax Museum at Buena Park where wax film dummies were everywhere, even sitting at tables at the coffee shop.

On our way to Palos Verdes, Uncle Necio asked me what I had liked the best so far. That was easy. It was the place where they prepared olives that we went to by accident. Uncle Necio had been looking for a place that supposedly had tame Japanese deer, but instead we ended up with a bunch of Japanese tourists who were being given a guided tour of olive preparation facilities. Uncle Necio groaned, but I found it fascinating, especially learning that black olives had that color because they were exposed to air, and the green olives weren't.

"You mean I take you all over Los Angeles to do some of the most exciting things in the city, and your favorite place was where they make olives?" Uncle Necio laughed.

"The other places were fun, too," I said seriously, "but I always wondered about black and green olives." Uncle Necio laughed again and dropped his new nickname for me of "Tight Money" for the good old standby of "Mr. Serious."

We went to Palos Verdes to see the stranded *Dominator* that had been abandoned the year before. From on top of a cliff we looked out to see the huge ship tilted in the water, stuck in a reef, I guess, waves pounding its hulk and spewing white foam.

"Isn't this more interesting than looking at olives?" my uncle kidded me. I had to admit it was more interesting.

We did so many fun things that Rita was back before I realized it. A week had gone by as if it had been two days.

It had been a while since I had seen Rita as happy as she was when she got back from visiting Halcy. As a surprise, she brought me a pile of comic books to make up for the ones she had thrown away. She thought that the tears that came to my eyes were tears of joy. I never explained to her about my love for Los Angeles, and how she had unwittingly put a tragic end to it when she had thrown the orange crate and comic books into the trash.

"We're moving, Michael," she said as I wiped tears away. And then she gave Uncle Necio a sad look.

"There are only three weeks left in the school year," Uncle Necio protested. "Besides, you move too much. Think about Michael for a change."

"We're moving for the last time," Rita said hugging me roughly. And then the shocker came. "We're moving to Yuma."

"Yuma?" Uncle Necio shouted. "You're crazy."

"I really am," Rita said letting go of me and looking at my uncle. "The world knows I'm crazy, you know I'm crazy, I know I'm crazy, and maybe even Michael thinks I'm crazy. How about it, Michael, you think I'm crazy?"

I stopped thinking of Los Angeles, Los Angeles with her bright orange sombrero, her inviting smile, her juicy oranges. The sadness I felt and projected was for her cruel fate, ending up abandoned in a dump, to be faded and torn apart by the elements or crushed under tons of garbage. Until the very end, she would blame me and think I had deserted her and doomed her to that awful fate.

"Don't be so sad," Rita said. "Wait 'til you get to Yuma. You'll see how you like it. We'll be living with Halcy. Remember how much you loved Halcy? You cried so much when she left."

"With Halcy? Didn't she move there to get married?" Uncle Necio said.

"It was that dumb magazine article saying there were so many single men in small towns. It didn't say why they were single. None of them are worth marrying. I told her it was a mistake. And then she was so ashamed of how things had turned out that she made it seem in her letters that the man thing was working out. But in a better way, things have worked out real well for her. She's running a small print shop, actually she's buying it. The man she was working for got ill, and so she's running it all herself, and he's letting her pay so much a month to buy it from him." Rita caught her breath. "She needs help, and she wants someone she can trust. So she offered to make me a partner. Can you believe it?" There was a look of disbelief but also joy on Rita's face.

"You don't know anything about running a print shop," Uncle Necio said looking as tired and exasperated as I had ever seen him look.

"Neither did Halcy, and look at her. I helped her while I was there, and I was picking it up."

"It's a real mistake," my uncle warned.

By this time I had put my comics on a chair, and I was fully immersed in their conversation. It was getting through to me. We were moving, but not to another place in Los Angeles. And what stuck in my mind was that we were going to live with Halcy. I loved Halcy. I had cried when she left, just like when I lost my dear, sweet but tragic Los Angeles.

"Yuma?" I said and both Rita and Uncle Necio looked at me. "We'll be so much happier, Michael," Rita said. "And Halcy needs us. She's so lonely. We had such a great time together. And she kept asking about you over and over. And she kept staring at your picture and kissing it. She really loves you, Michael."

I thought of Halcy with her short, curly blond hair. Of how she loved to joke and always had a glowing smile—for me anyway. And I thought of when Halcy hugged me, the perfume she wore sometimes smelled like oranges. And I thought of her orange-shaped face, and I thought, Halcy is Los Angeles, she's not at the bottom of tons of garbage, she's in Yuma!

My face brightened as I thought of our future with Halcy.

Rita and Uncle Necio stayed up late arguing about the move. I fell asleep to the rising and lowering of their voices. When I woke up, Uncle Necio was gone, and Rita was sitting at the table drinking coffee almost as if she hadn't gone to bed. But she was wearing different clothes, and her hair looked washed and combed.

"What time did you go to bed?" I said, putting my box of cereal on the table. And then I remembered it was a holiday, and Uncle Necio had said he was going to take me to Disneyland, but maybe he wouldn't feel like it now that we were moving to Yuma.

"I don't know," Rita said. "I guess it was late."

"Uncle Necio?"

"He slept on the couch. He was gone when I got up. He's sure mad about us moving. I don't blame him. God, we'll miss him. And what's he going to do without us? I told him he could marry Halcy." Rita laughed, but it was a laughter that verged on tears.

I brought a bowl and the milk to the table.

"Poor Uncle Necio," I said. Actually that was the first time I had given his welfare any thought.

Rita didn't say anything, but I noticed how furrowed her forehead was. And for the first time I noticed the lines coming out of the corners of her eyes. And I thought, how did Rita suddenly get so old?

"Did Uncle Necio say anything about taking me to Disney-land today?"

Rita took a thoughtful sip of coffee. "I wouldn't count on it." And then she took another thoughtful sip.

I dug into my cereal and ate slowly.

After I finished eating, I sat on the porch with the comic books Rita had bought me, and I waited for Uncle Necio to come and take me to Disneyland. Rita was in the house packing, and I was regretting that I hadn't laminated Los Angeles like I had meant to do so many times. That way I could have kept her close to me at all times. I would have had someone to talk to and someone whose love I knew was unwavering. By lunch I began to hate my uncle Necio for having abandoned me.

Pito ✧

1

"You come back again," says Pito, "and bring your girlfriend with you."

As we reach the door I turn to Pito, "She's not my girlfriend." I look at her, and I'm turning red. She looks at me blankly.

"Then why don't you stay?" Pito says to her. "You won't mind, will you?" he says to me with a face I can't decipher.

"But I gotta take her home," I say.

"No problem," says Pito, "I'll take her home." Pito looks at her confidently. "You staying?"

She's considering but shakes her head no.

As we go down the stairs, I turn to her and say, "You were tempted to stay with him, weren't you?"

"Uh huh," she says. That's all I get from her all the way back to her place.

When she gets out of the car, I feel like yelling after her, but she doesn't turn to look at me. Not even a good-bye.

2

I don't know why I bring these women to see Pito unless it's because none of them like me. They always want to go to a party or a bar, but I hardly ever have money. And Pito's the only friend I got. If you want to use the word loosely. And he knows it. He knows he can abuse our friendship or whatever you'd call it. So when the women are getting real bored with me, I always say, "Let's go see my good friend Pito. He's always up for a party." This never fails to cheer up my dates until we get to Pito's place.

He tries to score with every woman I bring over, but he's a dwarf, so he doesn't get far.

"If he had a humped back," one woman said, "then maybe."

We sit around drinking tequila or beer, and the women are usually yawning and looking at their wristwatches.

"So, Pito," I always say, "what's happening?"

"Nothing," Pito always says in return. His eyes always on the women. He almost always just talks to them. When he's talking to me, he's looking at them. Normally they don't like it much.

"Let's get out of here," they'd say in the beginning whenever Pito would go into the bathroom. After coming back to an empty apartment a couple times, Pito wised up and stopped going to the bathroom. Instead, he squirms like a kid.

When we're getting ready to leave, Pito always asks them to stay and go to bed with him. That gets the women out of his apartment as if he had yelled fire.

"Why are you like this?" I ask Pito when we're alone. "I don't bring these women over so you can score with them. They're my dates, but after you pull your number on them, they never want to see me again." But it's as if Pito doesn't hear me.

"Next time you come over," he always says, "don't forget to bring a woman. And try to find some good looking ones. The last ones you brought by were dogs."

3

"Take my picture," says Pito.

"Why?" I ask.

"So I can give them to your girlfriends," he says.

"They're not girlfriends," I say. "You have to see them more than once to call them girlfriends." I wince saying this.

"So what are they?"

"Strange interludes," I say really meaning it.

"Is that like intercourse only kinky?" Pito snickers.

"That's all you got on your mind?" I say.

"The women, they love me," Pito responds.

"So, why don't I ever see you with any? Why am I always having to bring women over so you can get your eye full?"

Pito looks at me morosely.

"You ask too many questions. So why didn't you bring any women tonight?"

"I met this woman at the laundromat." Pito's all ears. "She starts up a conversation when I'm putting my clothes in the dryer. She keeps talking to me while she's folding her clothes that she's taken out of the dryer. When she gets to her panties she presses them with a hand and folds them neatly. Sometimes she holds one up and stretches it with her hands and goes on about how she sure loves pretty underwear." I pause to get the optimum effect on Pito. He can't believe what he's hearing. He's practically salivating. I know he likes to look out his apartment with binoculars, but he almost never sees anything. During the daytime I've seen him pointing his binoculars at underwear on clotheslines.

"Why did you stop?" says Pito. "Tell me more."

"She tells me that she's just moved to town, and she's married, but she likes to go on dates when her husband's out of town driving a truck, which is most of the time. Anyway, I invited her to come see you, and she said she'd meet me, but she didn't show up. That's why I was late."

Pito is truly disappointed after the build up I was giving him.

48

"Forget the married ones," Pito says disgusted. "They're too complicated. Ain't you meeting any single women?"

"Single women?" I exclaim recalling too many painful experiences. "Either they're single and screwed up or married."

"I see," says Pito, "but crazy's not so bad. I heard about these teenagers who picked up this girl high on acid in some park. They took her to their place, and every one of them had a turn with her."

I don't know why I keep coming here. He can be so disgusting, almost demented at times, and he's always got such a smug smile thinking he's such a lady killer. But he can't even start up a conversation with a woman. He just stares at them. All that does is give them the creeps. I should tell him sometime. Oh, hell, why bother.

4

"I promise," I say to Pito, "next time I'll bring a woman."

"You bet you will," he says, "otherwise I got no use for you."

"Why don't you pick up some women on your own?" I say, finally getting a little fed up.

"I'm a dwarf," Pito says, "I can't pick up women except dwarf ladies. I don't want that kind. Their stubby fingers are a turnoff."

I stare at his stubby fingers but don't say anything.

"I almost got a woman to come over," I say teasing Pito.

"What do you mean almost?"

"She couldn't find a babysitter."

"You should have told her to bring them. I like kids. Why don't you call her? Tell her to come right over."

"They're teenagers," I say laughing.

"Teenagers don't need babysitters."

"I'm pulling your leg, Pito. Where's your sense of humor?"

"That's not funny. You driving me crazy, man. Telling me about a woman who would have come. Who would be here right now. Something beautiful for me to look at. Instead, I gotta look at your ugly face. You sick, man."

I get up to leave.

"Look," I say. "Are you my friend or not?"

Pito gives me the bum's rush to the door.

"Sure, sure, I'm your friend," he says as he's pushing me out the door. "But next time don't come without a woman." Pito slams the door.

5

I've never known a dwarf before, and I'm sure most of them are fine people but not Pito.

He calls me on the phone.

"Hey, I haven't seen you around lately."

"I haven't met any women lately," I say. "You said not to show up without any women."

Pito grows real quiet.

"Maybe you could come over once without a woman," he says.

"You really mean it?"

Pito grows real quiet again.

"What's your problem?" he finally says.

"What problem?"

"Why aren't you picking up on women anymore? A while back you were showing up with a different woman every week."

"Those kind of women weren't any good for me. They only went out with me because they didn't have anything better to do."

"I liked them," says Pito.

"I know you did."

Pito grows real quiet again.

"I gotta go," he finally says.

"So, you want me to come over?"

"Can't you hire a woman?"

"Hey, why don't you look in the classifieds. You can hire a woman yourself."

"Oh, man," Pito groans just before hanging up. "And you wonder why you ain't got no friends."

6

"I want you to meet a friend," I say to Pito as he opens the door. "Pito, this is Myrtle. Myrtle, Pito."

Pito's eyes are glued on her. Myrtle turns to look at me. She gives me one of those looks I'm used to getting: If you don't take me home right now, I'll scream.

Pito grabs one of her hands and yanks her in. Myrtle is too startled to scream. I close the door behind me.

"It's hot outside," I say trying to get a conversation going.

Pito's trying to get Myrtle to sit on his bed which is always a mess. His place is an efficiency. The only other places to sit are two rickety orange crates. Myrtle prefers to stand.

"Excuse me while I make the bed," Pito says. The sheets look like they haven't been washed in a while. There are some dark stains on the pillow case that look like dried blood. Pito sometimes gets nosebleeds when he's sleeping. He wakes up choking on his blood.

Pito's idea of making the bed is smoothing out a few bumps.

Myrtle turns to look at me.

"It's like an oven in here," she says, giving me an anguished look.

"Maybe a beer will cool us off," I say. "I'll get us some beers."

The refrigerator's empty except for a jar of mustard and a package of tortillas.

"I thought you was bringing the beer," Pito says sitting at the edge of his bed.

Myrtle has edged her way to the door.

"You taking me home?" she says half demanding half pleading.

"You sure?" I say.

"Take me home right now!" Myrtle is on the verge of hysteria.

"I gotta go," I say to Pito. "I just wanted you two to meet. Maybe we can all be friends."

Pito's eyes are still glued to Myrtle. He's licking his chops. Myrtle opens her mouth to scream. I knew it was coming.

7

"This is Monica," I say to Pito. "She's a beautician."

"I can see that," says Pito, "she's one great big beauty."

Monica is chewing gum, but she's not smiling like she was when I knocked on the door.

"Monica is into group sex," I say as an ice breaker.

"Not with a dwarf," she blurts out, looking at Pito then me and back again.

"You never tried it?" says Pito. "You'll like it." Pito's smiling his biggest smile.

"That's not what I meant," I say to Pito. "It's just something Monica was telling me as we were driving over."

"Yeah," says Monica, "but when you told me about your good friend who can't get enough of women, I thought . . . Hey, wait a minute! What did you bring me here for, anyway?" Her gum peeks out of her mouth and quickly disappears. "I'm going home," she says so emphatically that the chewing gum pops out of her mouth.

"I thought we'd sit around and shoot the bull," I say.

"Bull to you," Monica says.

"Yeah," says Pito. "I don't want to just sit around talking. Not with a beautician around."

Monica opens the door and is gone.

"Hey," says Pito, "someone should go after her."

But we don't move.

"She won't get a taxi out here," I say. "She'll look out at the dark desolate streets and think maybe it's not so bad up here."

"You think?" says Pito.

"I think." And as I say that there's a knock at the door.

"Remember," I say to Pito. "You get out of line, and I'm taking her right back home."

"I don't understand you. You bringing all these women over to tempt me and that's all?"

"Let's shoot the breeze," I say opening the door. It is Monica, and she's as white as a ghost.

8

"You see what happens when you let strange men pick you up?" I say to her. She's trembling by the door. Seventeen and beautiful but stupid.

"I like her," says Pito stroking her arm.

"Lay off," I say. "Can't you see she's scared shitless."

"What's to be scared of, deary?" Pito says, looking into her eyes.

She turns to me in desperation.

"I gotta go home," she says. "My parents will be worried."

She had told me she was living alone.

"We're going," I say to Pito.

"Not so soon," Pito pleads.

She's wearing shorts and a skimpy blouse. He's feasting his eyes.

"Look," I say. "She's going to die she's so scared. I'm taking her home."

She can't believe what she's hearing. She gives me a grateful look as we go out the door.

Down at the car I say, "You want to go dancing?"

"Sure," she says. The tension on her face relaxing. "You know something? You're sexy."

I just smile.

9

I bring twins over to meet Pito. I thought they'd go for him because they're short. But not as short as Pito. At 4'10" they tower over him. They look at each other and give each other identical looks. I wonder what their looks mean. Probably the same old stuff.

"You're ready to go?" I ask.

They look at each other and give each other those same identical looks.

"What do you make of it?" I whisper to Pito.

"I think they like me," he says.

"Both of them?"

"Sure. What's not to like doubly?"

It turns out to be a fun night. They stay for hours, not saying much but looking beautiful. That pleases Pito. But they don't spend the night. I don't know any woman who's ever done that. Driving them back home, I wonder which one of them I'll kiss. Maybe both.

I park outside their place.

"Well, fun night."

They look at each other and give each other those identical looks and then they burst out laughing.

"It was that much fun?"

They laugh all the way to their door.

You ever tried to kiss someone who's laughing?

10

"The dogs are barking in the city tonight," I say.

"And the cats are meowing," Pito says.

"How true. Dog and cat city it is."

"Yeah, gone to the dogs," says Pito.

"And the cats," I add.

"Sure enough."

"I love the city."

"Animal city."

"It's got teeth," I nod.

"For sure," says Pito. "You gotta watch your ass."

"True enough."

"Screeching nights."

"Wild."

"Beastly."

"And this is the city we love," I say.

"Wouldn't change it for none other," Pito says.

11

Pito's talking all night. His tongue in rhapsody. Conductor Pito, hair flopping with the excitement of talking, like a crow in its death throes.

"Long ago I came to this grimy old city . . ." says Pito when suddenly he gets a thought, "Why don't people cook these city pigeons with so many of them hopping around and so many people going hungry?"

"Correct me if I'm wrong," I say, "but maybe they don't taste too good. Maybe they're more feathers than meat."

Well, we soon forget all about pigeons, and I listen to Pito drilling and buzzing away with ideas. A fountain of wisdom. His language is rhythmical like ocean waves. And all night long I hear car tires driving through the wet streets, the sounds coming through the open window, and it's like a musical accompaniment to his talking.

Pito's putting straight all that is crooked with the world. Or in his words, "Even if it's made of steel, I'll straighten it out."

12

How did I land in this city? Pito wonders. How did I land in this room? A coffin room. Hardly enough room to turn around in even for Pito.

He's been stuck in this city for twenty years. Born in Mexico, he's never found anything better than this city, this room, an efficiency.

How did I land up in this life? Pito wonders. In this dwarf's body. Not my body, Pito thinks. A real mistake he's been paying for all of his life. I never bargained for this, Pito thinks and wonders how it could have been different, where in time it could have been avoided. His parents meeting?

Pito laments that his youth is gone. All of life's avenues seem to have led to a dead end, to an old and dying city. And Pito is growing old before he can figure life out. What good would it do, anyway? he thinks, late as it is. But wasn't it too late even from the start? That's a thought that keeps Pito awake many a night.

13

"Time is what you make of it," I tell Pito. Pito gives me a disgusted look. The kind of look he gives me when he wants me to stop talking. "Time is good times," I say.

"Say what?" says Pito, the look on his face going from disgust to revulsion.

"Time plus time," I say, "equals good times."

"You're crazy."

"I love time like a lady, Pito."

This is too much for Pito. "Where are the breasts of time?" he yells. "Where are the thighs of time?"

"You're my friend . . ." I start to say when Pito gets up to leave.

"I got no more time to waste," says Pito, "not with a crazy man."

"Time's not wasted on friends."

Pito shoots me a look that could freeze water.

"I'm leaving," he says as he heads for the door.

"I had a good time," I yell after him. But he doesn't turn around.

After he's gone, I go to the refrigerator and get myself another beer. I sit down and sip my beer and think of all the time I have on my hands. Plenty of time to do anything, but I'll probably just sit around drinking beer.

14

"Pito, why did she kill herself, such a beautiful woman?"

"Who's that?" says Pito.

"The photographer I'm always talking about. She listened, Pito."

56

"Listened? To who?"

"Anybody talking to her. She would have even listened to you, Pito." I smile, trying to show Pito I'm half kidding.

"What are you saying?" Pito's getting riled. "People listen to me."

"Who? Who ever listens to you except me and the women I bring over? And they don't like listening to you, Pito. And they never come back, Pito. They only come in the first place because they don't have anything better to do, and they don't know anything about you except what I tell them. I always build you up. But you're always a great disappointment to them, Pito. It's your personality. Face it. I'm the only friend you got. Just like you're the only true friend I got."

Pito can't believe what he's hearing. I've never talked to him like this before. He's momentarily stunned.

"You can't talk to me like this," he finally says.

"You mistreat me all the time," I say. "What do you mean I can't talk to you this way? I can talk to you any way I please. You never listen to me. You only want me around to hear you talk and to bring you women. And when I bring women over, I never see them again. You're always insulting them, making indecent propositions, leering at them, pretending to accidentally brush against their private parts. You don't even take the time to get to know them. It's your personality, Pito. You just don't care anything about anybody but yourself."

"Get out of here!" Pito screams. "I don't want you in my place no more."

"I'm going," I say. "Nobody is preferable to you."

Much later I get a call from Pito. I answer the phone groggy from sleep.

"Man," he says, "if you'll bring a woman over soon, I'll forgive you. Bring that photographer you're always talking about."

I shake my head not sure I'm awake.

"She's dead."

"Dead?" Pito grows silent for a while. "What do you mean dead?"

"Dead is dead. I gotta sleep, Pito."

"But you said she'd listen to me."

"You really don't listen, do you?"

"Oh, man, I'm tired of listening. I need some action."

I hang up on Pito and disconnect the phone.

15

Pito had a dream that Diane Arbus came to his door. I had been showing him a book of her photographs earlier that night.

"She said that she saw me walking in the park and so she follows me," Pito says. "Almost as soon as I get home, I hear a knock on the door. I open the door and there's this skinny woman with all these cameras hanging from her neck. I almost slam the door on her thinking she's selling cameras. But then she says, 'Can I come in,' and her voice is so sexy that I think, maybe I can get her to bed if she thinks I'm gonna buy a camera. When she gets in the apartment, she surprises me by saying she wants to photograph me, and I say only if I'm naked. And she says that's how she wanted to photograph me. I couldn't believe my ears. I was throwing off my clothes fast before she had a chance to change her mind. You gotta go to bed with me afterwards, I said. 'Sure,' she said as if that's what she had expected to do. I was out of my clothes in no time flat. And then she says, 'I can't photograph you with a hard on. This is for a magazine. They won't publish it.' And I tell her I always got a hard on when I'm naked around a woman. And then she says, 'Let's sit and talk until it goes down.' So we sit down on the sofa, and I don't know what to say. Finally she says, 'Tell me about yourself.' And while I'm talking, she's rummaging through my dresser drawers poking her nose into everything. She even finds the porno magazines. 'Do these do anything for you?' she says. She flips through them. And then she says, 'They don't do anything for me.' You won't believe this, then she says, 'You should see the photos of genitalia I have. I'll bring them over sometime.' I was too stunned to tell her to stop poking her nose into everything. But then I found myself getting mad that she was invading my privacy that way, and I found myself yelling at her to leave. Can you believe that? She was gonna go to bed with me, and there I'm yelling at her to leave. 'But I haven't taken your picture yet,' she said. I had to push her out the door, and after I locked the door, I noticed all her cameras had fallen to the floor. And she was banging on the door screaming for her cameras, calling me every obscene name she could think of."

"I can't believe it," I say. "Even in your dreams you can't score. And as horny as you are. What a shame."

Pito seems embarrassed that he told me about the dream.

"When I woke up, I was sweating. It was such a real seeming dream. I looked all over for her cameras and was relieved not to find them. But then I thought, I really blew it. This normal woman wants to go to bed with me, and I kick her out. If she had only stuck to taking my picture and left my life alone. It's like she was getting too deep. It was real scary. I was hating her."

"It was just a dream," I say. "In real life I bet you would have gone to bed with her."

"You think so?"

"I'm sure of it."

"Let's look at that book again," Pito says.

"I left it at home. I'll bring it next time."

"Let's pretend you brought it," says Pito.

"Alright," I say, and I pretend like I'm opening the book of Diane Arbus's photographs. "That photo," I say, "people would spit at it when it was first shown at the Museum of Modern Art." I point at the empty air.

"I can believe it," says Pito. "Let's get to my picture."

I go along with Pito. I pretend like I'm turning some pages.

"Stop," says Pito, "there I am."

I look closely at nothing.

"What do you know," I say, "that is you."

"She only photographed me from the waist up," Pito says disappointed. "I don't know why she was waiting for my hard on to go down."

I pretend to close the book.

"It was only a dream, Pito."

Pito shakes his head. "You saw my picture, didn't you? How could it have been a dream then?"

"But you said she didn't get a chance to take your picture."

"I lied. She did take my picture."

We grow quiet.

"You say she killed herself?" Pito finally says.

"Yeah. Killed herself."

"She didn't have any friends?"

"I don't know why she killed herself."

"I should of gone to bed with her," says Pito.

"Maybe you'll dream about her again," I say.

"That's just dreams," says Pito.

"You gotta be alive to dream."

Pito thinks about that.

"You mean dreams are real?"

16

In this dream, Pito and Diane Arbus go out for a cup of decaf and a roll someplace.

"You're not drinking your coffee," Pito says.

"That's okay," says Diane, "I just want to hear you talk."

"How about your roll? You eating that?"

"No, you can have it. I'm too sick to eat."

"Sick of what?" Pito says.

"The doctors don't know. I think it's the birth control pills and the hepatitis I had once."

"You're taking the pill?" Pito leers at Diane.

"I've lost eight pounds," Diane says as she fidgets with the lens on one of her cameras.

"You wear those cameras around your neck as if they were charms or holy medals," says Pito.

Diane looks up at him and smiles wryly.

"Maybe they are."

"You're the sexiest woman I've ever known," says Pito craning his neck. She's let her miniskirt slide back far enough for him to see her panties. And then Pito is blinded by the flash of Diane's camera.

"Not again!" says Pito.

Diane keeps clicking her camera. She gets up and takes shots of him from all different angles.

"Not tonight," Pito pleads, but Diane doesn't listen. She's possessed. Click, flash, click, flash. "You're blinding me!" Pito yells.

Pito wakes up to the bright light of morning hitting him in the face, and he's in bed, alone.

17

In this dream, I drop by at Pito's with Diane.

"Pito, this is Diane Arbus, the famous photographer."

"I know," says Pito, "we already met."

"Hello, Pito," says Diane, smiling at him as if they're old friends. I turn to Diane.

"Why didn't you say anything?"

She doesn't answer me. She just looks at me and smiles.

"Pito has a great place, don't you think?" she says.

I look around. The place is a mess. There's something on the table grown moldy. The floor's deep with socks, underwear, magazines, and newspapers.

"Well, it's small," I say, "and it's a mess, but I like it."

"I pose for her nude sometimes," says Pito. "She followed me home once, and she said, 'Take off your clothes, I want to take your picture.' And I said, 'Take off your clothes first.' And she did, so I did too."

"I'm really disappointed," I tell Diane. "I was really hoping to introduce Pito to someone new."

"So," says Diane adjusting one of her cameras, "how about if I take some pictures? Why don't you stand next to Pito?"

"With our clothes on?" says Pito.

"Wait a minute," I say, "this isn't my idea of fun. I thought we'd sit around drinking some beers and talking."

I open three beers from the six-pack I brought, but Diane doesn't want hers.

"Come on you two. Get closer."

I'm getting nervous. Pito's getting nervous. I walk to the door.

"I'm leaving," I say.

When I wake up from that dream, I call up Pito.

"Hey," I say, "remember all those dreams you've been having of Diane Arbus? I'm starting to have them now."

Pito's unnaturally quiet. Finally he says, "You go to bed with her?"

"Nawh. I took her over to meet you, but it turns out you both already knew each other. And then she wanted to take our photo together. That's when I left, and I woke up and called you."

"That's good that you didn't go to bed with her, otherwise you wouldn't be able to get her out of your mind. I'm going crazy when I'm awake. I just want to be asleep and dreaming about her."

"You've gone to bed with her?"

"I think so," Pito says. "When I wake up, I don't remember all the details." A pause. "But I'm not stupid. Now that I think of it, I'm sure I've gone to bed with her many times. Otherwise why would I be so disappointed when I wake up? And why would it be eating me up like it is?"

"She's something, isn't she?"

"The best," says Pito.

18

"Pito. The wine does flow."

"It does flow under the bridge and the barges flow on it, and the wine flows out to the sea, and the world flows away."

"Sure," I say, "that's how it is. What's the news with Diane? Have you dreamt of her lately?"

"I dream of her constantly. I don't know if it's real or not."

"I envy you."

"You with real women! You envy me!" Pito exclaims. "She's just a dream woman," he says faltering.

"It's all dreams," I say. "Life is all dreams. You haven't told me how it's been with Diane lately."

"It's good. It's always good. Even when it's bad, it's good. Better than hanging around with you just drinking wine."

"Where is that bottle?" I say, feeling thirsty. Pito hands me an empty bottle. "You went and drank all that and didn't even save me a little? What kind of friend are you?" I throw the bottle across the room. It bounces around but doesn't break.

I don't drink that much, really, except when I'm around Pito. And he claims he hardly ever drinks either, except when he's around me. We wouldn't have anything to say to each other if we didn't get half drunk.

19

"I'm in and out of love in a day," I tell Pito.

Pito shrugs. Except for his dreams, I doubt if Pito's ever been in love. I doubt he's ever even kissed a live woman. I'm not insinuating he kisses dead women. He likes them hot. That's what he says. And in his dreams, someone like Diane can be blazing hot. There are advantages to a dream life.

In dreams, love goes on and on for lover boy Pito.

20

James Dean comes to Pito's door with a camera.

"Hold it," says Dean, an unlit cigarette in his mouth. He clicks the camera. "No film," says Dean looking at Pito. "Next time I'll take a picture of you with film." Dean looks down at his camera doing something.

"I thought you were Diane," says Pito staring at the camera.

Dean looks up astonished, the cigarette almost falls out of his mouth.

"Diane Arbus?" asks Dean. Pito nods yes. "I've been looking for her to give me lessons."

"She's dead," says Pito possessively. "She don't give lessons anymore. She just takes pictures and then she leaves you all alone, and you feel like you're dead."

"That's how you feel?"

"Sure, that's how I feel. I feel dead and used by her. She just wanted my picture. She's got that, and now she's gone."

Dean looks at Pito sympathetically.

"You really thought I was her? You were hoping, weren't you?"

"The camera is all I saw when I opened the door."

"You wouldn't mind my taking another picture?" asks Dean.

"You said you don't have any film," says Pito.

"That's true. It's real amazing," says Dean.

"What's amazing?"

"Diane being dead." Dean opens the back of his camera. "Yep, no film."

"It happens every day. People dying."

"Oh, yeah. Hold it!" says Dean. "This would make a great picture." He focuses the camera and clicks.

Pito smirks.

21

"Pito, you're my friend."

"Sure, sure. I'm as much of a friend as you'll ever have."

"That's all I need in this dream life," I say. "Like old Kerouac said, 'Life's a dream that's already been lived.' "

"Carrot who?"

"Kerouac. A writer who died in 1969."

"You're always bringing me down," says Pito, "talking about all these people who are dead and done. First there was Diane. Now it's Carrot-ac. Why aren't you bringing no more women around? Real living women. Not dreaming of women. Like you were talking to me about Diane, and I end up dreaming of her for weeks and weeks. Real seeming, yes, but dreaming of women ain't the same. You pinch them, and you wake up."

I continue in the same vein as before, saying how Kerouac had said this and that. The next day I see Pito, and I say, "What's happening, Pito?"

"You know who I seen last night after you left?"

I look at him surprised.

"I didn't know you had any other friends but me."

"I was dreaming," says Pito. "What do you mean I ain't got no friends? I got plenty. Too many as a matter of fact. You're one of my excess friends. I could drop you like this," Pito snaps his fingers, "and I wouldn't even notice you were missing."

"Right, Pito." I laugh. "Tell me about this dream."

"It was that Carrot-ac guy you were talking about. He knocks on the door, which is confusing because I begin to wonder am I dreaming or not. And I yell, 'If you don't got a woman, I don't want to see you,' thinking it was you. But then I hear this voice. Out of curiosity I open the door. Not the real door, but this red door in my dream. And this guy barges into my room. He's carrying a big bottle of wine, and this black girl trails after him. She's beautiful. I can tell that right away even though I didn't turn on the light. And Carrot-ac says, 'We heard Diane's here.' And I say, 'She was here last night, but I don't know what's happened to her. I think she's gone for good.'

"I lied. I hadn't seen her in weeks, and I keep hoping all the time she's coming back any minute. I move closer to the black girl since it's dark, and I'm thinking I can get a feel, and she won't know who did it. But she sees me, and she moves away. And Carrot-ac says, 'You mean we've come all this way for nothing?' and he takes a swig from his bottle of wine, but he don't offer me any. And I say, 'You want me to give her a message if I see her?' hoping that'll get rid of him, but Carrot-ac doesn't say anything. He just walks over to my bed and falls asleep, the bottle of wine clutched tightly in his arms. Then the black girl says, 'I see he's moved in with you. Thank goodness. I've had enough of him and his crying all the time about his mother. How she does this for him, and how she does that for him, and how I don't do nothing for him. I let him in my bed. That's more than I shoulda done. He's your misery now.' She heads for the door, and I yell, 'Hey, what's this about? I need some sleep. Where am I gonna sleep?' The black girl turns and laughs. 'If you can find Diane, have her take his picture then he'll leave. Otherwise he's gonna be with you a long time.' I feel frustrated, but I'm still attracted to her, so I grab one of her tits, and just as fast she kicks me in the groin. I wake up having to go to the bathroom bad. So, you get me out of this mess you got me into."

"What mess?" I'm astounded by what Pito's been telling me.

"When I go to bed again, I'll have to get out of bed because Carrot-ac will be there snoring and smelling like a bum off the streets."

"Maybe he'll be awake."

"Even so," says Pito, "that black girl said I'm stuck with him unless Diane takes his picture, and I'm afraid Diane's gone for good."

"He's one of my favorite writers," I say. "I'd give anything to meet him. Especially since he's been dead so many years. I'd like to hear what he has to say about death now that he can talk about it firsthand."

"Fine," says Pito, "when I go to sleep tonight and I'm dreaming, I'll tell him to freeload on your dreaming."

"Do that Pito. Tell him I'll help him find Diane. I want to ask him more about life being a dream. Don't you ever feel like it's all been done, and we're just dreaming it?"

Pito shakes his head in disgust as he often does.

"When you coming over with a real woman? No more dream ones, please, and definitely no more men."

"Pito, you're my friend?" I find myself saying this from time to time because of my feelings of insecurity.

"Yeah, yeah, I'm your friend," says Pito with a pained expression on his face. "But you better hope that Carrot-ac freeloader migrates to your dreams; otherwise, I don't ever want to see you again."

After that meeting, I don't see Pito for a long time. All the women I keep meeting seem like they've been dreamed up and are not really there. At first, Pito calls me all the time saying, "Aren't you bringing any women by?"

And I tell him, "I meet these women who keep disappearing."

Most of the time Pito slams the receiver and that's that until he calls again. But when he doesn't hang up so fast, I ask him about Kerouac.

"He still hasn't entered my dreams," I tell Pito. And Pito always says the same thing. "He says he's writing a novel, and he won't leave my bed until he's finished or until Diane shows up. So every dream I land up sleeping on the floor. And when I wake up, I feel like I really did sleep on the floor. I'm going crazy, and it's all your fault." And then Pito slams the phone.

Finally, I go see Pito even though I can't get a woman to come with me. Pito actually seems grateful to see me. From the door I can see Kerouac on the bed writing furiously in a little notebook. Piles of little notebooks are all around him. The floor is littered with empty wine bottles. Kerouac is concentrating so hard on his writing that he doesn't even look up to see who's at the door.

"You see, Pito, life is all dreams."

Pito turns and gives Kerouac an anxious look. Kerouac lifts up his head and squints in my direction.

"Where's Diane?" Kerouac says.

"She's dead," I say, thrilled to be talking to such a famous writer.

"So am I," Kerouac says nonchalantly as he pulls out a bottle of wine from under a blanket. I notice it's one of the cheapest, and strongest, wines you can buy. He unscrews the cap and takes a long drink as if it were soda. "So where is she?" he says as he screws back the cap. Kerouac stares at me. I'm beginning to feel uncomfortable.

"You see," says Pito, "it's been like this. I ask him things, and he don't answer. When he does talk, it's to ask about Diane. Otherwise he just writes in that notebook or sleeps. Where he gets all this wine and those notebooks, I don't know. He never leaves the bed. I'm dreaming, aren't I?" Pito gives me the same kind of anxious look he was giving Kerouac earlier. "You've come knocking in my dream, and I open the dream door thinking you're Diane. . . ."

Just as Pito says her name, we hear a knock at the door that makes us all jump, including Kerouac sitting on the bed.

"You want me to open the door?" I say. It's just right behind me. I don't even remember having closed it.

"It's gotta be her," says Kerouac, putting down his notebook and unscrewing the cap to his wine bottle. I've never seen Pito looking so distressed.

"This is my dream!" he screams, "and I'll open my own damn dream doors."

Just as he's about to open the door, I wake up because the phone is ringing, and I have been dreaming all this from the beginning. But it's not really dreaming, it's living. Without even picking up the phone, I know it's Pito. I look at my alarm clock. It's five in the morning, and I know he's been up all night. The room is dark, but as the phone keeps ringing, the room seems to be getting darker. Finally I pick up the phone.

"Pito," I say not giving him a chance to speak. "Are you still my friend?" But there's no answer. Just the silence of darkness and the long distance across telephone wires. "Pito," I say again, my voice trembling this time, "I knew from the beginning this was all dreaming, what we call living." Still no response. Just the dark silence. And then I suddenly think, Diane! It's Diane calling. "Is that you? Is that you, Diane?" The silence is frightening.

"Diane's here," Pito says, his voice sounding old and tired. "You want to come over?"

I hesitate before I answer.

"Are you dead, Pito?"

"We're all dead, don't you remember?"

I don't say anything but stay listening to the static on the line. And this goes on for over an hour, an infinitely long hour, before Pito finally hangs up.

22

"Diane? Where is Diane?"

"Her body was rotting when they found her. Wrists slit. Pills in her tummy," says Pito.

"I should kill you!"

"Try and you're dead. I'll cut you in pieces." Pito reveals a switchblade almost as big as he is or so it seems.

"I don't like how you've been talking about Diane," I say.

"What you gonna do about it?" Pito's taunting me, waving his knife in front of my face. "You could take a wrong step and get cold steel in you."

"You're a dead man, Pito. Not tonight, but some night."

"We're all dead men some night," Pito laughs a chilling laugh.

23

Diane's knocking on the doors of his dreams all night long.

"Pito, let me in."

He hears her stricken voice, and the knocking is louder each time. Mountains of knocking. And he's afraid to answer, because he knows Diane is dead, and there's nothing he can do about that. What is it that she wants from him?

"All I ever wanted is to take your picture," she says through the cracks of the door. "Open up, Pito; I will do anything you want. Anything to take your picture." Her voice is desperate, and she is crying.

Pito is terrified of this deathly voice and of his dream room and the dream doors that resound louder and louder with their impossible demands.

When Pito wakes up, he never wants to go back to sleep. In the beginning of his love affair with Diane, he could accept that she was dead. But dreams, he had thought, should be safe. Safe to love the dead in dreams. Now he knows there's no safe place, and dreams are worst of all.

24

When Pito tried to kill me with his knife, a long switchblade that slit my side, but not bad, just cut the flesh, bled worse than it was, I knew it was because he was crazed with Diane and the wine of a long night gone to the dogs. I promised to kill him in return. I thought I could do it, but then I thought, what would I

69

do? Cradle him in my arms with the life seeping out of him and no scotch tape or any glue to hold it in? I could kill him, I know, but then where would I be? But I promised him and all because of Diane. We love her too much. A dead woman!

When Pito came at me, I could see myself dying and Pito yelling at me as my slippery blood poured out on the floor like the flowing blood of slaughter houses. Him yelling at me, "You're going to her, aren't you? You son of a bitch. You pushed me to kill you so you'd be with her."

"Pito, I love her," I'd say. "You don't know love." And as I was dying, "You never loved no one. Not even a dog, much less a woman."

I saw all that coming as he lunged at me with his brilliant knife. But it was only a flesh wound.

"You got yours coming," I yelled tripping him to the floor and getting out of there fast.

"You're dead," I could hear him yelling after me, then his sobbing.

That night I dreamt of Diane. "You two were fighting for me, weren't you?" she said. I didn't need to answer. She knew. She placed a hand on my bleeding wound that was flowing like a river. I couldn't believe how deep the wound was. Her arm went all the way in. And then all of her disappeared into my wound.

"Diane!" I yelled, "Get out of there. That's my wound, not yours."

She had gone into the hurt that had become unbearable. So unbearable that I could have killed myself to end the pain. There was a knocking in that dream.

"I know she's there," Pito yelled when I didn't open the door. "Let me in."

I gave a frightened glance at my wound, but there was no trace of Diane. I had no intention of opening the door or even of saying a word.

The knocking grew louder on my dream door, in my dream life. Is there any difference between waking and sleeping?

"Diane," I whispered to the deep inside of me, "I know you're there. Come out. How can I live with so much pain?"

70

Pito's yells from beyond the door were fading away. "What'd you do with Diane?"

I couldn't help smiling. Even with such intense pain, I was at peace.

Las Vegas, Las Vegas ✧

It wasn't until I was eleven years old that I realized that Las Vegas, New Mexico, and Las Vegas, Nevada, weren't one and the same town. This realization came about real slowly and took me several days of standing out in freezing temperatures before I wised up. It was the week I waited for days outside the El Fidel hotel to see the couple arrive who had won an all-expense paid trip to Las Vegas. We had gotten our first television set a few months earlier, and I would have watched TV every possible minute if my mother had let me.

A frequent prize on a few game and quiz shows was a trip to Las Vegas. I had never thought of my hometown as being an especially desirable place and certainly not a place people went out of their way to visit, much less a vacation destination. It was alright for the people who lived in it, but it seemed to me that it would be too small and quiet for anyone else. But the people on TV jumped up and down with what at first seemed to me an excessive display of joy. You could tell tears were rolling down their smiling faces when they wiped them away with the backs of their hands. As I saw this exuberance repeated on TV program after TV program, I began to suspect that there was a side to Las Vegas that totally escaped me.

One winter afternoon I posted myself across the street from the El Fidel hotel in New Town not giving a thought to the fact that it was one of the coldest winters on record. The night before I had watched a young couple on a game show go crazy with happiness when they were told to pack their bags because they were going to spend a fun-filled week in Las Vegas. I figured that they couldn't possibly arrive in Las Vegas any sooner than the afternoon of the next day. The hotel was just a few blocks from the train station, and I figured they'd be whisked over to the hotel in a taxi. I'd recognize them as soon as they stepped onto the sidewalk because they would look like people looked on television, not a weird look, but a special look, a television look. And of course they'd be smiling and looking happier than anyone else who had ever lived. And they'd have a ton of luggage. I thought that by seeing them in the flesh, I would somehow come to understand what it was about Las Vegas that the world at large found so appealing. The Las Vegas everyone wanted to visit. The Las Vegas with a glitter and shine like a dime I had put mercury on once to make it look new to give as a present. That special Las Vegas that had so far eluded me even though I had covered all of its alleys and back streets. But those people from the game show didn't show up.

Three straight days I went back to the same spot across from the El Fidel, and they never arrived. I was certain they didn't, because the El Fidel looked just as drab as it always did, and I knew that if those two people had arrived, their presence alone would have transformed the hotel, would have made it brighter and bigger. Everyone going by on the sidewalk would have had big smiles because Las Vegas was a fun place to live in, and everyone would be deliriously happy that they lived there and didn't have to go through all the trouble of winning a quiz show or game show just to spend a week or two there. No, the hotel was unchanged. And Las Vegas was the same unexciting place. I was greatly disillusioned, and I suspected there was a great lie somewhere. Could television be perpetrating a great lie about Las Vegas to a gullible country? I wondered. If so, what happened to all those contestants who won trips to Las Vegas? Were we, the inhabitants of Las Vegas, the ones who were living the lie? Was there really a greater, shimmering Las Vegas out there?

And then I learned that there was a Las Vegas in Nevada, and that was the one people in television were always going to. I decided that was the Las Vegas I wanted to live in, the Las Vegas the whole country was interested in. Those of us in Las Vegas, New Mexico, were living a lie. No one in the country cared we existed. One day I received a giant Sugar Daddy in the mail. I had saved the required number of wrappers and sent them in, but the Sugar Daddy sucker was first sent to Las Vegas, Nevada. That was the second thing I noticed when it arrived in the mail. The first thing I noticed was that it had been opened and then poorly taped back. That convinced me, even the United States Postal Service wasn't convinced about our existence.

When I go to Las Vegas to visit my mother, I usually take her out to eat. One visit not long after I had turned forty, we happened to be driving across the Gallinas River (Chicken River) when my mother turned to face me, smiling as if remembering a pleasant moment, "Remember," she said, "when you had that tree house?" When I was twelve or thirteen I did have a tree house, and it had been just a short distance from the bridge we crossed. It was near the railroad tracks not far from the river. It startled me to hear her mention the tree house because I couldn't remember ever having told her about it. Also, and I found this equally startling, the act of crossing the bridge had also caused me to think of the tree house, and we were probably thinking of it at the same instant. It was something I had not thought about in many years.

"It must have been pleasant," she said as we turned the corner where the recently renovated two-story building stood, the one that always used to stink. There was a sign that said it was a gallery, but the few times I had gone by it it always seemed empty. When I went by that building a few months later there was a "For Lease" sign in a window. For years there has been some attempt to invigorate the economy of Las Vegas by fixing up some of the old buildings for new businesses. But empty buildings remain. Few new businesses last more than a year.

Las Vegas was stagnating long before I was born. I haven't seen much of a change during the twenty plus years since I left even though people in Santa Fe are always telling me that Las Vegas is the up and coming place with all its wonderful old buildings and cheap rent. But few of those people have ever been in Las Vegas, and if they have been there, it was only for one or two short visits. They believe the articles they read in the Santa Fe or Albuquerque newspapers that feature the new look that Las Vegas is taking on. But the articles are always overly optimistic. They are written by people who only spend an afternoon in Las Vegas and who believe everything they're told. Or even if they don't believe it, they realize what they were told will make a good story.

Besides my mother, I still have family members in Las Vegas. I've left it for good as far as my living there, but I go back often to visit, and I drive around and see newly fixed up buildings with broken windows and other signs of vandalism, and I'm overwhelmed by a feeling of sadness. And I think, nothing has changed.

I think hides were stored in that stinking corner building. It always smelled of things rotting. I remember passing it with friends, and all of us closing our noses with our fingers. But there was one time I passed by it when I didn't notice its smell. My nose had been bleeding; I was trying to keep from crying. I was walking and pushing my bicycle along. Rómolo was not far from me. I felt angry and betrayed by him—my anger was directed towards the boys I had fought with, towards Rómolo I felt disappointment. In the back of the *Daily Optic* where we picked up our newspapers to sell for six cents on the New Town street corners, I had gotten in a fight with someone I had accused of removing a screw from my bike. It was a new bicycle. We got in a fist fight, and all the other kids formed a circle around us. As soon as I was winning the fight a couple of his friends hit me from the back and on the side until he got the upper hand. Rómolo hadn't done anything to help me. I realized then he wasn't a friend. We walked to Old Town not saying a word. I can see us as we passed that building with the terrible smell of desiccating animal skins. And for the first time and the only time, I didn't smell that horrible smell. The blood was clotted in my nostrils, and I was angrier and sadder than I had ever been.

It surprised me to hear my mother say that she thought it must have been pleasant having a tree house. I had never thought of it that way, but when she said it, I realized it *had* been pleasant. Only, I had thought it was my complete secret. I couldn't remember having told any of my friends about it. Why would I have told my mother? Could I have told her long after the fact? I don't remember. But I do remember using the thick railroad tie nails I found along the tracks to make a ladder up the tree. The fork of the tree where I made my tree house was quite a ways from the ground. The long square nails I pounded into the tree made a great ladder. I spaced them far enough apart that they weren't too conspicuous, and I don't think anyone ever noticed them—or if they did they found it too perilous to climb—because there were never any signs that anyone had climbed up to it. If someone had, they more than likely would have trashed it. But it was always as I left it. I loved climbing. Being small and thin, it took hardly any effort for me to climb up the nail ladder. I'd sit in the tree house by myself for long periods of time. I was far enough from the traffic going across the bridge that I hardly ever gave it any notice. I seldom saw people passing below me. But anytime anyone went by, they never noticed me. I was quite content.

Sometimes my friends and I would sneak through the bushes along the Gallinas River hoping to find college students from Highlands University making out in the grass. I've forgotten who the other kids were who I went with, but we usually never saw anyone. The few times we did find college students lying in the grass, the most they were doing was kissing. The stories we had heard had suggested much more, but maybe the word got out to the college students that the grass and bushes along the river were thick with kids anxious to spy on them. I say river, but at many places along it, it was easy for a kid to jump across, or at places there were rocks you could step on to get across.

At one time someone dammed up part of the river, and the spot became a sort of swimming hole. It wasn't wide or deep enough to really swim in, but then most of us didn't know how to swim anyway. We mainly splashed around and had water fights and sometimes sat on and pushed around the crude raft that must have been left there by whoever had dammed up the river. And if the swimming hole and raft hadn't been made for us, it didn't matter, because we enjoyed them just the same, and no one ever came along to chase us away. But there had been one close call one day when I dove off the raft like others had been doing. The water was murky, and when I surfaced, I came up underneath the raft. I hit it so hard that the impact stunned me, and I immediately went back down. When I came back up, I was choking on water and flailing about desperately. The other kids gave me a funny look puzzled by my behavior. It had felt like I had been close to death, and because of how murky the water was, none of my friends had had the slightest idea what was going on under the surface. Finally, a flood washed the dam away, and no one built another one. By that time our interest was elsewhere.

If I were to now walk the distance from where I lived to that river, I know it would be a very short walk. But back then it seemed far away. Maybe it was because along the way there were lots of things of interest that kept my attention. There was the irrigation ditch just across the street from my house. It was a place of constant interest with or without water. When there was water, we caught water spiders, which were skiing about on the surface of the water. And there were minnows and tadpoles. At one time I even kept tiny snails in a large jar that I found in the ditch. There was also slimy moss we'd scoop up and throw at each other. When the irrigation ditch was empty, it was a hidden place to walk through, and there were always things to find there that had been left by the water. But we always had to be on the lookout for a man who acted like he owned the ditch and would come after us with a stick if he saw us. We didn't see how it was possible for any one person to own the ditch, and we thought he was crazy. Even if someone had proven to us that he owned the ditch, there wouldn't have been any way to keep us away permanently. But each time we saw him, he did manage to scare us off for a while. In our minds, he wasn't just crazy but also possibly an ogre, because the only place we ever saw him was in the ditch or along it, and we had read fairy tales about ogres and trolls living under bridges. We never did see him up close or get more than a glimpse of him before we took off running. Not getting a good look at him added to our suspicion that he wasn't human.

Sometimes at night we'd get the courage to go along the irrigation ditch looking for La Llorona, a woman our parents had warned us about. She had drowned her children in the irrigation ditch, and she was there at night looking for other children to drown. There were a couple nights I thought I heard her as I was lying in bed with my open window facing the irrigation ditch. Her cry was sort of like the cry of a cat but with more of a human sound to it, sometimes like the crying of a baby. We were able to build up our courage to go to the irrigation ditch at night because it was the perfect route to take to raid fields and gardens. We'd run off to the river with our arms full of ears of corn and cucumbers and carrots and even sometimes a small melon. And in the thicket of trees along the river, we'd make a fire where we'd roast the corn while munching on small cucumbers and carrots. I think the only other people who ventured along the river at night were winos who would go there to pass out drunk. We never saw them, but in the daytime we often saw their empty wine bottles and signs of their small camps.

I said the irrigation ditch was the first distraction on the way to the river, but really the first distraction was the street right before the irrigation ditch. It was where the young kids of the neighborhood were always playing: games of baseball with a folded sock and a stick, touch football, hide-and-seek, races, or just standing in the middle of the road and waiting until cars got close to us before we scattered in different directions yelling at the tops of our lungs.

Once the road and irrigation ditch were crossed, there was what seemed to be an immense expanse between the ditch and the beginning of the trees that lined the river. The land sloped down from the ditch to an empty field, but in the summer when it was overgrown with weeds that were taller than we were, it became a jungle, a place where we dug tunnels through the undergrowth and followed endless trails that went in a myriad of directions. There were grasshoppers to capture and watch spit their tobacco juice. There were large weeds with stalks as thick as our arms that we'd decide were enemy soldiers or monsters, and we'd attack them with our wooden swords and hack at them until all their limbs were gone and the stalk was brought to its knees. In the fall, the people who owned the field would gather the weeds into piles and burn them. I think the smell of weeds burning in the fall is one of the best possible smells. And in the winter, the field was the perfect place to make the biggest imaginable snowmen and impregnable snow forts, which we'd defend with our stockpiles of snowballs that had rocks in the middle. At least two of the many scars on my head date back to those snowball fights.

To the right of the field was where the junior high and high school were located. The junior high was a two-story adobe building that looked its age. It was built in the late 1800s by Jesuits as a college, but then they abandoned it to move the college to Colorado. The school grounds had many black walnut trees, and in the fall the ground would be littered with nuts. I'd take large bagfuls of them home and end up staining my hands black from peeling off the skins. I'd eat a lot of them in my backyard breaking them open by hitting them with rocks.

There were locust trees along the irrigation ditch above the school grounds. In the spring they were full of blossoms that were sweet tasting. Somehow the word got around from kid to kid which plants were edible, and in the course of a day and during the right season, we'd snack on two or three different wild plants. One that I especially liked was a weed that grew flat along the ground and was full of tiny green fruit shaped like tires or round pillows. They had to be peeled open, and it took a handful to get more than a taste. There were also small bushes that had fruit that looked like tiny tomatoes not much bigger than peas. When I was real young I ate elm leaves until I saw a green worm doing the same thing.

Outside the building where they taught woodworking was always a pile of sawdust and discarded pieces of wood that seemed to me to have endless possibilities. In between the junior high and high school, there was a small rock building shaped like a cave. It had a rounded cement roof and the inside was empty. It might have been left over from the days of the Jesuits and could very well have been a place where a statue of the Virgin Mary was placed. I only think of that now, that it might have been a grotto, but back then it was a fun place to climb because the outside walls were of rough rocks with plenty of places to get a hold. I got into the habit of climbing it and jumping off into a pile of sand until one day I hit my chin with my knee while I had part of my lip between my teeth. I bled profusely and never jumped off again—off that building anyway.

Between the high school and the river was the football field, which for a long time was just dirt and rocks and toritos. Toritos, little bulls, is what we called the many-sided thorns that grew there in profusion. When I was older and played football there, we'd start each football season by crawling back and forth across the field gathering all the thorns we could find. But it was impossible to find them all. All football season we'd fall on them. Our opponents dreaded playing on our field, and we relished the thought that they'd get to enjoy our toritos.

To the right of the weed-overgrown field was the junior high and high school and so many things. I haven't even mentioned the gigantic pile of boxes that'd be gathered for the homecoming bonfire. We'd crawl through the pile and make temporary club houses out of the bigger boxes.

To the left of the field were a couple of large vegetable gardens and the parochial school known as the Sisters' School. I remember a little gang I belonged to hiding in the trees and undergrowth that bordered the Sisters' School playing field. We waited until the unsuspecting kids had come out for recess and had gotten into their games, and then we charged at them screaming and waving our wooden swords, routing the kids back to the safety of their buildings. At this point the nuns would charge after us waving their rulers in the air to match our swords, their black habits flapping in the air. We would retreat back to the dense growth along the river where we knew no one would follow us.

Whenever I cross the bridge from Old Town to New Town and I see the narrow band of trees growing along the river, it never fails to amaze me how few trees there are compared to what I remember. And when I cross the bridge when the leaves are gone, I get a glimpse beyond the trees and see the field and the land sloping up to the irrigation ditch. I know the ditch is there by the line of trees growing along it, many of them locusts, and I think what a short distance it is, but it wasn't always that way.

I grew up in a city divided. The dividing line was the Gallinas River, also locally known as the Frijoles River or the Tortilla Curtain. The city voted to consolidate a few years after I left for college. I jokingly thought it ironic that they waited until I left to consolidate, and I wondered if my leaving had anything to do with it. Of course it didn't, but I found it amusing to think so. When I was growing up, each side of town had their own mayor, police department, fire department, public school system, and other functions a separate city would have.

I grew up in Old Town or West Las Vegas. Across the river was New Town or East Las Vegas. East Las Vegas came about when the railroad decided to put its tracks a couple miles east of the plaza, which allowed a new town to spring up. Politics as always were involved. Politics was the one word I always heard while I was growing up. It was what put a lot of money in a few pockets but otherwise left things the same, if not worse, for everyone else.

The railroad came to New Mexico around 1879, but almost twenty years earlier Las Vegas was already a bustling town. The Santa Fe Trail went through it with a heavy traffic of stagecoaches and wagon trains. As an important trading and shipping center for a wide area, Las Vegas was one of the fastest growing towns in the territory at a time when Las Vegas, Nevada, was nothing more than a ranch.

When I was growing up in the 1950s and 1960s, West Las Vegas was in a stupor and had been in a stupor for a long time. It was as if the town still hadn't gotten over wondering what had happened to the Santa Fe Trail, and there were still grumblings about the politics that had been involved in putting the railroad tracks east of the plaza. People spoke of things that had happened sixty and seventy years in the past as if it hadn't been that long ago. People still spoke of Billy the Kid spending the night in the Las Vegas jail, of hangings, of vigilantes, and of outlaw gangs.

One of the outlaw gangs people spoke of most often was the Vicente Silva gang. You could sometimes hear a twinge of fear in their voices when they recounted some of his heinous deeds. They spoke of Vicente Silva as if he were someone they had known and under whose terror they had lived. Silva was shot in the head in 1893 by one of his gang members shortly after he killed his wife with a knife. He wasn't killed to avenge her murder, his gang members weren't of that sort, but for the money belt and the jewels he had in his possession. There were still people living who could remember the Vicente Silva gang from when they were children, but most of the people I heard tell the stories were telling stories that had been passed down from family member to family member. After sixty or seventy years, the stories still brought fear to young and old alike.

When my mother first moved to Las Vegas, I think she lived in East Las Vegas in a house not far from the railroad tracks. I was a baby when she moved her family, my two brothers and sister, to West Las Vegas not far from the river. I vaguely remember that house. What I mainly remember is a tree of green apples, eating some and getting sick. It's when my mother moved to the first house we lived in on Gonzales Street that I start having any clear memories.

The house on Moreno Street was the last house I lived at in Las Vegas. It was directly behind the south end of the Old Town plaza and just around the corner and a short walk from the two houses I had lived in on Gonzales Street—they were only a few houses apart. On Moreno Street, I lived a house away from the two-story building that people claimed had been Vicente Silva's saloon. Like many of the older buildings in Old Town, the two-story building was connected to a series of adobe homes; they stretched to the corner of Moreno Street and South Pacific Avenue and then down South Pacific Avenue. In the old days people built houses one room at a time and hence

82

the reason for their long and narrow shape. But houses built that way very often didn't include halls, so to get from one end of the house to the other, you had to go through every room in between. With time, after the original tenants died or the family sold the property, many of the houses were divided into several apartments. The first place I lived in on Gonzales Street was like that. The main part of the house was long and had a front facing South Pacific Avenue, and from a corner a small wing went straight back facing Gonzales Street. The woman who owned the house lived in the large section, and she divided the small wing into two apartments. An old man lived in a one-room apartment, and my family lived in a two-room apartment at the end. There were elm trees in the yard, and that was where I got into the habit of eating elm leaves.

It was commonly thought that there had been many tunnels radiating from underneath Vicente Silva's saloon going in all directions. Most of them were said to be for escape or to hide his booty, but one of them, so the story went, led directly underneath the bank, a short distance away at the east corner of the plaza. Though people often talked about those tunnels, no one ever claimed having been in one or knowing anyone who had been in one. In an empty lot not far from Silva's saloon, the earth would mysteriously collapse from time to time leaving behind small craters. All the kids in the neighborhood were convinced this was evidence of Vicente Silva's tunnels. Adults shrugged their shoulders and weren't sure. The two-story building, which only consisted of two rooms, had been abandoned for a long time. Finally, the apartment next to it was abandoned and allowed to fall into disrepair, so much so that the owner finally tore off the roof and pulled out the vigas which had carvings on them. He had them lying around in the yard for a long time until I guess he sold them.

The old saloon and the abandoned apartment were divided by a hallway. It wasn't a hallway built inside a home, but a hallway that separated two buildings. The kids of the neighborhood were in and out of those rooms all the time, playing games and exploring. One day a friend and I noticed that some of the planks on the hallway floor seemed loose. We pulled them up easily and found a small space under the floor. My friend and I looked at each other and immediately thought the same thing: the tunnels! We went back to his house for a flashlight, and I crawled into the hole. The hole was just barely big enough for me to crawl through but very quickly it opened into a basement. There I was able to stand up. The floor was littered with what looked like old whiskey bottles. There was a door to a safe, and stuck in one of the dirt walls was the frame for a door. It was funny to see it there leading nowhere, the opening filled with dirt. I crawled out and told my friend what I had seen, and we were certain the doorway had led to a tunnel that had caved in. He declined crawling in to check it himself. I never crawled back under the building because the man who owned it started checking up on it more often. And someone told my mother I had been under there, and she almost got hysterical thinking of me crawling in a dark hole full of creeping things. I've often wondered about that underground doorway leading nowhere. Was that Vicente Silva's secret tunnel? If so, the stories about his many tunnels seemed greatly exaggerated. And the door to the safe? Where did that come from? All the liquor bottles certainly confirmed the story about the building having been a saloon.

Growing up in Las Vegas in the 1950s, I've told people before, was like growing up in the 1930s in other parts of the country. When I say Las Vegas I mean West Las Vegas, and I mean the neighborhood bounded by South Gonzales Street to the east, Moreno Street to the north, and South Pacific Avenue to the west. In the south, South Gonzales merged into South Pacific. When I was very young that basically contained my whole world. That and the stretch of land that dipped down from South Gonzales to the Gallinas River. And also the plaza which South Gonzales and South Pacific fed into right past their intersections with Moreno Street. A year ago I walked the loop around that neighborhood. It took maybe a half hour or so of leisurely walking with a number of stops. I thought it might be important to take some photographs, which I did. I have those photographs, looked at them a few times, but they don't do much for me. I've come to realize the important photographs are in my head, or more accurately, they're like movie clips that I occasionally set going in my mind or that run by themselves triggered by a smell, an image, a thought, a sound. They're always little snatches of my past beginning and ending abruptly. There is no one long movie of my past, I've come to realize; there are only fragments.

I think my family once lived on Alamo Street, but it's when we moved to South Gonzales that my memories truly began and, in a sense, so too my life.

Before my mother got an icebox, we would leave our perishable food items outside on the window ledge. I still have a mental picture of a bottle of milk, butter, and something else outside the window on the snowy ledge. I don't know what we did in the summer, though it probably was more of an inconvenience than a serious problem considering we didn't have that many perishable food items. Our main food staples were beans and potatoes and red chile. My mother would sometimes make bread, as well as tortillas, that she'd keep in a bread box. Any bread or tortillas that became too dried out and hard were fried in a pan. I thought it was delicious, a sort of toast. I'd sometimes fry it on my own. Or if we had milk, it was usually dried milk, she'd make a pudding with the old, hard bread.

When we got an icebox, it required going to the icehouse to get a large block of ice. The icebox was a simple operation. You put in the block of ice, and that was it. No electricity needed. Early on, my two older brothers must have gotten the ice. I don't remember. But I remember when I was six or seven going for ice at the icehouse across the Gallinas River and across the railroad tracks to the New Town side (I didn't really think of East Las Vegas starting until I had crossed the railroad tracks) and bringing the ice back in my little red wagon. It seems to me that early on my wagon had a covering, a miniature version of the canvas coverings the horse-drawn wagons had in the Old West days.

My mother would sometimes tell me about traveling with her father from Chacon to Las Vegas in a wagon. The eighty miles or so round trip would take at least two days. They'd spend the night by the railroad station where a lot of other wagons would park. She'd sleep under the wagon making a bed out of the blankets she had brought for that purpose.

Once in a long while relatives passing through town would stop by and leave us some food. Maybe someone would kill a cow on their ranch, and they'd bring us a few cuts of meat. Or during hunting season someone might kill a deer and bring us a piece of meat. Sometimes my mother would cut the meat in thin strips and hang it from the clothesline to make jerky. Other than that, we didn't eat meat too often. Hamburger was a treat and was usually made to stretch by mixing it in with beans and chile or with potatoes. The other major addition to our diet was "commodities." I remember standing with my mother several times in a long line outside a warehouse. My little red wagon came in handy for hauling back the commodities. Usually there'd be large containers of extremely sticky peanut butter, lard, dried milk, and I don't remember what else. If we were lucky there might be some butter and processed cheese. All the items came in government packaging which made everything look the same.

Early on my mother cleaned people's houses in New Town. Many of the clothes I wore until I was in about the fifth grade were hand-me-downs the people she worked for would give her. I remember her taking me to houses she worked at, and I'd sometimes play with the children whose old clothes I'd sometimes be wearing. There was always a distance between us, and they'd often give me a strange look as if there was something peculiar about me. The people my mother worked for were Anglos who I had never had contact with before except for my aunt Mary who was married to my uncle Moisés and was one of the few Anglos living in Old Town. But I didn't really think of her as an Anglo. What I saw as Anglos were people who lived in a world totally closed to me, except when my mother took me along when she cleaned houses, and then I painfully saw first-hand how truly different our worlds were. There were lots of Anglos in New Town, and the few houses I went into with my mother impressed me with their seeming wealth and abundance of food, anyway wealth in comparison to the life I lived.

We had a large radio that stood on the floor. I loved sitting on the floor and listening to it. I don't remember listening to music on the radio. When my mother listened to the radio, it was usually Spanish music (really Mexican music, but it was called Spanish music just like the meals of Mexican food that schools and various groups would have as fund-raisers were called Spanish suppers). When my mother put on her music, it was time for me to leave the house. I found the music terribly boring and time lasted forever when I had to listen to it. But then when you're young, time often passes excruciatingly slow, and there's so much boredom, especially when adults drag you along with them.

There was one radio program I especially liked to hear. I think it was called the "Supper Club" or something like that. The host would talk to people on stage and then he would go into the audience and talk to people at random. I could see it all in my head. And there was a comedy program on Saturday mornings that I'd rush home and listen to after getting out of catechism class. I found it extremely funny.

There weren't too many ways to make money in West Las Vegas, especially if you were a young kid, but every now and then I went around looking for soda bottles that I could take to grocery stores for their deposit. I also picked up wine bottles that I'd cash in at liquor stores. For awhile I made money selling popsicle sticks to a lady who made candied apples to sell. I'd wander both West and East Las Vegas looking for the used popsicle sticks. Eventually, she stopped buying them from me because she had more popsicle sticks than she could use. During the summer, I would sometimes get work pulling weeds. But that was hard, dirty work under the hot sun. What made it especially hard work was that by the time people were willing to pay me to pull their weeds, the weeds had grown into a forest with some stalks as thick as my arms. I remember pulling furiously at some weeds and having my hand slip. Sometimes a cut would appear on my hand similar to a paper cut, only deeper and wider. I still have a scar across one of my fingers. One pleasant though not too common dividend was that you never knew what might come up with the clod of dirt hanging to the roots. Usually an old penny, but once in a long while a nickel or a dime, and on occasion an old token. One token I found was good for a drink at the Plaza Hotel, and another one said it was good for a loaf of bread.

I can still remember losing a dime and the distress it caused me. It was outside Dick's grocery store, a one-room grocery store with a small wood stove in the middle. There were usually several old men at the store talking with Dick. When the weather was bad, they'd gather around the wood stove. But on warm days they'd sit on the porch and watch the traffic on South Pacific Avenue. The store was perched on the side of a small hill that rose sharply above South Pacific. There was a metal handrail in the cement steps that rose up to the porch of the store and sometimes I'd hang out there with other kids. We liked to hang from the bar which was difficult to do because it was at a sharp angle. I'm surprised Dick never chased us away from there, but he was very easy going. One day I was hanging on the bar and had a dime in my shirt pocket, that was a lot of money to me. It might have been something my mother's boyfriend of that time had given me. Most of the extra money I had came from her boyfriends. A nickel here, a dime there, and some Sundays a quarter to go to the movies. I could make ten cents stretch a long ways. Dick had a large selection of penny candies. There were some taffy candies that were four for a penny, and others that were two for a penny. Anyway, I decided to hang upside down even though it was awkward to do because of the angle of the bar. Once I was hanging upside down, I saw my dime fall out. The dime fell where Dick threw cinders from his wood stove. I quickly got off the bar and searched through the cinders, but the silver dime disappeared in the white cinders. Generally, I was good at finding things on the ground, and I must have looked for over an hour until I gave up. That was a hard loss to take. It took a lot of soda bottles and wine bottles to get back that much money.

There were times I was so hard up for money that I'd wander all over Old Town and New Town looking for it on the ground. By the end of the first day I had found over thirty cents. One nickel I had to dig out of the asphalt in the road. I searched alleys, parking lots, sidewalks, and street water drains where I'd use a stick with some chewed gum at one end. But after that first day, I seldom found much.

When I was old enough, I sold papers on the street corners in New Town, but there were lots of kids doing the same thing, so I never made much money. When I was older, I tried a couple paper routes. The first one I did I had to sign up my own customers. I think the most customers I ever had including the Sunday customers was maybe sixteen, and they were spread from one end of Old Town to the other. My mother made me quit the route when the winter became especially cold. The other paper route belonged to a friend. I helped him for a while, but he hardly paid me anything, so I gave it up.

I dimly remember when my mother signed up for welfare. I remember going with her to different offices and being deathly bored with having to sit for hours in one waiting room after another. But the welfare wasn't approved until she talked to a politician or two, and when my mother heard it was approved, the look on her face made it seem as if she had accomplished the impossible. Cleaning houses didn't come close to paying the bills, not to mention buying food, especially with four children. We had been receiving commodities for years, which was a sort of welfare, but then we started receiving a check. It wasn't much money, but the main difference was my mother was able to spend more time at home looking after her family, three boys and a girl. Our monthly eating cycle didn't change much. We ate alright for the first half of the month, but from the middle of the month until the end of the month, the amount of food and selection of food got progressively worse. From the middle of the month to the end of the month it was mostly commodities. I remember all the food running out and only having lard to eat spread on a stale piece of tortilla. Those were the times we'd fry any piece of hard bread and tortilla that might still be around. Sometimes there'd be a jar of mustard, and I considered a mustard and tortilla sandwich to be a great treat. But by the end of the month there wouldn't be any tortilla to spread it on. The last week of the month usually meant going to bed hungry. I can remember crying in bed and not being able to go to sleep from the hunger I felt.

Across the fence lived two sisters close to my age. They'd get me to play house with them by tempting me with real food, a piece of candy or a slice of baloney. I'd be the husband, and all

I'd have to do was sit around and wait for them to serve me dinner. But first they'd pretend to be doing housework, and then they'd look after their dolls. I was always impatient for them to hurry up and get to the part when they'd serve me dinner. But they wouldn't be hurried. There was the imaginary tea to be poured and other dumb things I glumly endured.

My mother's last boyfriend worked at his family's small grocery store on South Pacific a short distance from where we lived on Moreno Street. The store was called the Square Deal and that's where we did most of our grocery shopping. His name was Carlos, and I remember always seeing him in the meat section cutting meat. He had been married and had a son and daughter who he had brought up in California. His son had stayed in California, but his daughter—extremely beautiful—was in high school at West Las Vegas High. From bits and pieces that I heard, I learned his wife was in the State Mental Hospital a couple miles outside Las Vegas and that it looked like it was a permanent stay.

His parents were an older couple with white hair. I would often see at least one of them in the store. They were always very pleasant, especially after their son started dating my mother.

Carlos was working as butcher at the store and taking classes part-time at Highlands University, a small college in East Las Vegas. His ambition was to become a teacher, which he eventually did. He moved to Albuquerque to teach and dropped my mother for an elementary school teacher who he married after a short romance. It was a shame. He had dated my mother for several years while he worked on his degree. She loved him and thought he felt the same way. Anyway, he died of a heart attack shortly after marrying the school teacher.

I think of his daughter every time I watch a certain television program on Saturday nights. The star of that program is married to Carlos's daughter. I read about it several years ago in the *Albuquerque Journal*. They were visiting Las Vegas, and he told the reporter he was thinking of buying some property there. I wondered who they were visiting in Las Vegas and if her mother was still in the State Hospital. I thought that if Carlos had married my mother, they might have stopped to see her.

After high school, Carlos's daughter went to Las Vegas, Nevada, where she became a show girl. A few times he proudly showed us photographs of her sitting with some famous star in a nightclub setting. By that time I fully understood that Las Vegas, Nevada, and Las Vegas, New Mexico, were two different places, but what continued to perplex me was calling a place in the Nevada desert "Las Vegas," which in Spanish meant "the meadows." Someone once explained it to me this way, "They call it the meadows because of all the green felt on the gambling tables, and all that money that changes hands. That's green, isn't it?"

That seemed like a plausible explanation, but still I had my doubts. What seemed more likely to me was that Las Vegas, Nevada, was named after Las Vegas, New Mexico. After all, Las Vegas, New Mexico, was one of the biggest and most prosperous cities in the territory long before Las Vegas, Nevada, existed as a town. This seemed like such an obvious explanation that it surprised me that I had never seen any reference to it. And then one day I saw an old map in a book that showed the Spanish Trail from Santa Fe to Los Angeles. And there in the area where Las Vegas, Nevada, now stands, the word "Vegas" appeared twice, referring to the area where the Las Vegas Creek flows out of the Las Vegas Springs. I realized there had been a marshy place there long before the city of gambling casinos and nightclubs was built over it. The Spanish Trail was in use from 1830 to 1848. Las Vegas, New Mexico, wasn't selected as a town site until 1835. Las Vegas, Nevada, wasn't founded as a city until 1905, but it was on the map since the early 1830s. That ruined my theory, but I found it intriguing to consider that some of those men who traveled the Spanish Trail to trade New Mexican handwoven woolen goods at Pueblo de Los Angeles, San Fernando, San Juan, San Luis Rey, and other California towns might have been some of the early settlers of Las Vegas, New Mexico. Stopping at that oasis around the Las Vegas Springs wouldn't have been something anyone would have forgotten. A place for their pack animals to recuperate after crossing the jornada de muerto, a fifty-five-mile stretch of desert with no source of water. The men must have bathed in the creek or the springs to get off the crust of dirt and sand from weeks of traveling. They were close enough to California that they could indulge themselves in the pleasure of imagining the cool sea breezes along the coast. And when some of those men were back in New Mexico and helping to build a new town along a creek with rich meadows, did they remember that other place also called "the meadows," las vegas? When they crossed the Gallinas River, did it remind them of the Las Vegas Creek and the oasis that grew around it? And did they remember what they thought when they crossed that creek? How the sturdy California mules and stock they'd be bringing back, traded for their New Mexican serapes and other handwoven goods, would be able to fill up on grass and water before the grueling trip back across the jornada de muerto, called the "journey of the dead" because of all the people who perished there. In more ways than I had ever realized, Las Vegas, Nevada, and Las Vegas, New Mexico, had a shared history and a common bond.

Carlos would always get angry whenever we'd play Chinese checkers and he'd lose, which was most of the time. He was determined to beat me soundly, so we played quite a few games over a period of weeks. But for every game he won, I won four or five. Finally, he gave up on Chinese checkers and started bringing over different board games looking for that one game that'd bring me to my knees. But I was adept at board games, and after a while he gave up on them.

I waited across the street from the El Fidel in the middle of the winter. I had my coat buttoned all the way to the bottom of my chin. I had a sweater on underneath my coat and my gloves on. Occasionally I'd try to thaw my ears by covering them with my gloved hands. From what I remember, the winters back then were much colder. The snow was deeper and lasted longer.

Around that time, it got so cold one night that all the small birds froze, or it seemed like all of them froze. One morning I woke up and my mother said it had been over 40 below that night. I bundled up and headed for the plaza. We lived directly behind the south end of the plaza on Moreno Street behind the Palms Ballroom.

When I arrived at the plaza, I saw a sight I had never seen before and never would have expected to see. The yellowed grass beneath the trees was covered with the frozen corpses of small birds. I thought of how I had slept undisturbed in a warm bed while the birds were freezing. I wondered if they gave off feeble cries when the cold got to the point of no return. It seemed to me that maybe I had heard their cries while I slept, though I had forgotten all about it when I woke up. Or had I forgotten? I had rushed to the plaza on an extremely cold morning with no special purpose, no special purpose I was consciously aware of. And then I witnessed the birds. It has never been so cold again in over thirty years.

I stood outside the El Fidel to catch a glimpse of the people I had seen on television, the couple who had won a trip to Las Vegas. I wanted, needed, confirmation that the place I lived in was known to the world, known and desired. People went into hysterics and burst into tears of joy when they were told they were going to Las Vegas. The whole country watched them on television and envied them.

The day after seeing them on television I was there, across from the El Fidel, waiting for them, the happily married couple. They looked happy on television. Maybe they weren't happy before, but after winning the trip to Las Vegas, they were the happiest married couple in the country. And who wouldn't be, getting an all-expense paid trip to Las Vegas.

If my mother had known where I was and what I was doing, she would have scolded me. "What are you doing standing there like a tontito in the cold?" A tontito, someone with absolutely no sense, and to make matters worse, putting himself on public display to show off his tontito-ness. But what else would you expect from a tontito? "Don't you know que la gente hablan?" She always worried what people would say, what people were saying behind your back. I didn't worry, but it was frightful to see the extent of her concern about such matters. I never told her, but I often felt like telling her, "Why do you worry what other people think? If they don't have anything else to do but bother themselves with other people's business, then they have pretty sorry lives."

I was quite certain that the El Fidel in New Town was the hotel they would be staying in. It was three stories high, and I think the only hotel in town at the time. The Plaza Hotel in Old Town, a grand four-story hotel that has since been restored and reopened, had been closed for a long time. I knew a boy who for years lived on one floor in the Plaza Hotel with his mother and sister. I never visited him there, but I think they lived on the second floor. I always wondered how many rooms they occupied, and I liked the idea of having a choice of so many rooms to live in. There were a few motels in town, but people winning a trip to Las Vegas would never be put up in a motel. I couldn't imagine it.

Each day the sky was a frigid blue. As I stood at my spot across from the El Fidel, sticking my gloved hands into my coat pockets and then periodically bringing them out to cover my ears, I remembered my mother saying to someone a week before, "At least it won't get too cold today with all the clouds in the sky." Each day I cast a despairing glance at the clear sky, a sky like a block of ice. Finally I gave up. It wasn't just the terrible cold that made me give up. I decided that something must have gone wrong. If they were coming to Las Vegas, they should have already arrived. All I could think of was that they had been mistakenly sent to the wrong place. But that didn't make any sense. And then I began to think, why would anyone be awarded a trip to Las Vegas, New Mexico, in the middle of the winter? Especially a winter so cold that all the birds had frozen. And I was filled with doubts: doubts about the reality of Las Vegas and, by association, doubts about my own reality. Could the people I had seen on television have arrived, unseen to my eyes? Could they have enjoyed themselves and then left, again unseen to my eyes? I had an eerie feeling not unlike the feeling I sometimes got watching the "Twilight Zone." Could there possibly be two Las Vegases, each existing in the same time and space, but other than that totally unalike with no possibility of interaction? It was a farfetched idea, but I had a vivid imagination.

94

✧ Getruíta

As I drove to my aunt's funeral in Mora, I thought of how cloudy it had become after days of the best possible fall weather. A cold front was moving in, the sky filling with wintry clouds. I kept glancing at my wristwatch every few minutes wondering if I'd be late for the 10:00 A.M. funeral mass, and I wondered if I shouldn't have brought a thicker jacket.

I thought of the plains which I could get glimpses of to my right during breaks in the pine forest. And I thought about how I had grown up in a country where the mountains and plains meet. Or it could be said where they part. When the road rose to a point where I had a good view of the plains, I thought how the plains looked like the back of a sea creature rising out of the ocean, its plain, smooth back in contrast to the wavy effect of the pines.

But mostly I thought of my aunt, Getruíta. She was the wife of my mother's brother, William. A few years earlier I had driven to Mora to his funeral mass and then to my aunt's house in Chacon after the burial. He had fallen off his tractor, and a wheel had driven over his skull. That was in Chacon, in a field across the street from his house. After his funeral, I found myself alone with my aunt in her kitchen. She looked out the kitchen window, across that road, and at that empty field. Without my prompting her, she told me how just a few days earlier she had been standing by the sink peeling potatoes, every now and then looking out the window to see her husband on his tractor. One minute she saw him out there working in the field, then she looked away, and when she looked back, he no longer was on the tractor. It was moving by itself. She didn't say anything more. She just kept staring out the kitchen window.

We had buried her husband hours earlier. The house was filled with relatives and friends of the family. People eating. Everyone else was in the living room, but I lingered with my aunt in the kitchen. I looked out the kitchen window to see what she was looking at. But how could I possibly see what she was seeing, looking as she was through eyes of sorrow and loss? And with a crushed heart as if driven over by a tractor? I followed her gaze and saw a road without traffic and an empty alfalfa field. No tractor, I thought. And I tried to imagine what I thought she might be seeing, a tractor with her husband on it, and then suddenly an empty tractor driving on its own power.

My uncle William and my aunt Getruíta were my godparents. They lived across the river from my grandparents' house, my mother's parents. I was born in that house. The earliest memory I have of it is of it being painted in polka dots, the only house I remember being painted like that. In a few years it was painted over in a solid color. Even as a child I thought the house looked a little odd—odd and whimsical, I think, looking back. The way I knew my uncle and aunt were my godparents was that one day when I was very young, they gave me a bag of candies. They had never given me candies before and never gave me candies again, so that memory stayed vividly in my mind. Over the years my mother would remind me that they were my godparents, and in case anything ever happened to her, they would take care of me. But as I grew up, I had almost no contact with them. When I was young, there were times I wished for another bag of candy. But when that bag of candy failed to materialize,

I would think about that one bag of candy sealing the bargain, their becoming my godparents, no reason to expect more.

Over the years I seldom saw my uncle and aunt. My uncle never attempted to have a conversation with me. And if I made an attempt, he abruptly brought an end to it. My aunt was more open, though we seldom spoke, and when we did, the conversations didn't last very long. But on a couple occasions, many years apart, I remember her face lighting up as she spoke of how clear and alert my eyes were when I was a baby. And when we would talk, I would sometimes feel that she was remembering that baby who she was convinced looked at the world with a surprising intentness. I think it made her feel closer to me in some way, even though over the years we never saw each other much. But I think she was also perplexed trying to reconcile the image of the clear-eyed baby and the grown man I had become. There were times I would find her staring intently into my eyes as if my eyes were an enigma she very much wanted to understand but knew she never would.

I pulled up to Saint Gertrude's church in Mora about ten minutes before the mass was to start. As I walked up the stairs, I remembered the dead bird outside my house a few days earlier. Wasn't that the same day my aunt died? I wondered. And as I was about to walk into the church, an older, thin man came up to me and started talking to me in Spanish as if he knew me. He looked like he had been drinking, not just that day but for a whole lifetime. I couldn't make sense out of what he was saying. And it wasn't until I got away from him and walked down an aisle that I thought, Celso! Years earlier I had written a book of poetry about a town drunk, philosopher, outsider, trickster. Someone who I had imagined living in a place like Mora, a small northern New Mexico town. Celso knew my aunt?! I thought in surprise. But then I thought, why should it be so surprising when Celso was a creation of my mind. He has come to pay his last respects, I thought, drunk as he is, and I felt touched but also perplexed. I had thought he was a product of my imagination, and yet here he was in the drunken flesh! At the end of mass, I noticed him as I walked out. He was smiling at me, and it was the kind of smile that seemed to suggest that he had the upper hand on me. He knew who I was; did I know who he was, his smile seemed to say. I almost went over to him. I wanted to ask him, "Are you Celso?" But then I thought, if he was Celso, he would enjoy confusing me by remaining cryptic.

At the burial, after the casket had been lowered and the soil was being shoveled into the grave, I made my way over to Lizardo. It was his mother who was being buried. We watched the dark soil being shoveled into the grave, and we both whispered our approval at how rich and dark the soil looked. "Do you see how there are no rocks in it?" Lizardo whispered with the appreciative eye of someone who had farmed for a living. I hadn't seen Lizardo since his father's funeral, and we whispered reminiscences about that one summer fifteen years earlier when I had stayed in my grandparents' house that had been empty for years. We whispered about what a grand time we had had. Going to dances. Drinking lots of beer. The comradery of those brief two months still vivid in our minds.

Lizardo spoke too of his mother, how she had suffered for a long time. How she was able to do less and less with time until she had to be bathed and dressed. How liquid would get into her lungs, and she would struggle just to breathe. He spoke of her coma and how she hadn't recovered from that. And now she was finally released from all that suffering.

Many people had come to the funeral mass and also to the burial. Earlier I had watched the sons and daughters, my cousins, standing close to the coffin while some words were being said by the priest. I watched the weeping and the sadness on the varied faces. I looked closely at them: Benny, Raymond, Priscilla, Edith, and Lizardo. And I felt close to them. Close in realizing they were my blood relations and in seeing such familiar features that were shared by other relatives. Close in seeing their grief and in seeing how they were letting go of a loved one, their mother.

She was buried in Chacon just a few miles from where she had lived. Chacon is at the head of a valley. A few houses denote a village, but the scattered houses down the valley are also Chacon. Just a few hundred people in the whole valley, El valle de San Antonio, Saint Anthony's Valley. Every now and then I would look away from my aunt's coffin and the people gathered there, and I would look up at the mountains rising sharply and look back at the sweep of the valley. I thought how dry everything looked this year. I thought how beautiful it was but austere and cold. I remembered that when I had been a child spending summers with my grandparents, Chacon had always seemed austere and cold, even on days when the sky wasn't filled with wintry clouds. I reflected that I was born in that valley but that I could never live there. I thought of life as being too raw there, too bone bare; that's how I remembered it from having spent time there as a child. So many years later, looking around the valley, I wasn't convinced life here was any different than what I remembered. I felt the weight of the mountains towering over an almost insignificant valley floor.

After the burial, people met in Mora, at a small building that was a recreation hall for senior citizens. I sat next to my oldest brother, and for some reason he started talking about the year I was born, something he had never talked about before. He was about eight, he said. They had gone to Chacon because there was no place else to go. My mother had moved her family of two boys and one girl from house to house in Las Vegas until there was no money left. And so she moved back with her parents for a year, the year I was born. There was no other place for her to turn.

I was born in the fall. We buried my aunt Getruíta in the fall. Buried her forty-two years and one month after I was born. As I drove back to Santa Fe I pondered the meaning of premonitions, of signs. And I wondered if the cold front, the wintry clouds, was a sign coming as it did after several of the best fall days. On the way home, I had a flat tire. And as soon as I got home I started coming down with a cold. Other signs? Not too significant as signs go. But maybe in the days to come there will be other signs. Or maybe in looking back I will come to understand certain premonitions. Try to find some meaning in this process of dying. And in turn come to understand a little better what it means to be alive.

Petroglyphs ✧

"Nearly two thousand of 'em, they've counted," she said.

I had hoped to avoid her. I saw her as I was walking down the hill. From a distance she had seemed like an old man. That's what I had thought. Some old-timer hanging out in the rest area waiting for someone to come along so as to talk the person's ear off. I had come over the crest of the hill where I could see the rest area about a quarter mile away. I had been hearing music as I drew closer. Horrible, I had thought, thinking how beautiful a place this was, so far from any town, yet there were some young men here with their radio blaring.

I had noticed them as I had driven up to the state park. I parked as far away from them as I could. They looked like they had just gotten up. I saw three of them. All of them with long hair that needed combing. They seemed to be trying to get a fire going. Empty beer cans scattered around their area. They had a makeshift tent set up. Just a couple blankets spread over ropes. It had been a frigid night. They seemed too intent on getting their fire going to pay much attention to me. They hadn't turned on their radio yet.

"Yep, nearly two thousand," she repeated.

There had been no way of avoiding her. From the crest of the hill I had searched for another way to the car. But it was all fence as far as I could see. The trail led to the only opening through the fence. And she was sitting only a few feet from that opening, sitting on the concrete bench next to the concrete picnic table. The tin roof sheltering the picnic table cast a shadow, so I couldn't see until I was half way down the hill that it was an old woman not an old man sitting there as if waiting for me.

I had thought I'd walk by her swiftly. Give a curt nod if she said anything and head directly to the car. But it was as if she had cast a net in front of me and pulled me in.

I turned to her and said, "What's that?" That was it. She wasn't going to let me get away easy.

"Nearly two thousand petroglyphs, yes sir." She said the word petroglyphs slowly and with importance as if it were a word she had long pondered and had concluded was a word of supreme significance. "I counted them myself," she said in affirmation.

I noticed the cap she wore had Tres Ritos State Park on it. That's all that gave her away as working for the park service. She wore old but regular-looking clothes. Her gray hair was short. She had the worn features of someone who's lived in the West all their life and has spent most of that time in the sun and wind. Looking at her skin I thought of trees with their bark worn off, but with the bark worn off so long that the weather has worn ribs and furrows into the tree making it resemble the bark again. I could see why I had taken her for a man from a distance. She had the general appearance of a man in his seventies who's overweight but not terribly so. She held on to a large stick that was propped up by her knee. It looked like something she had found and peeled and was using as a cane.

I looked back up at the hill where I had come from. I thought how over the top of the hill there were a couple other hilltops and ridges you couldn't see from this vantage point. I thought of the jumbled black rocks, volcanic, I had thought, and I thought of some of the petroglyphs I had seen, most of which I had seen by staying on the trail, but a few times I had gotten off the trail to get a better view of something. Immediately off the trail the ground was thick with plants and rocks with sharp edges. Just a few miles away I could see mountains rising to at least ten thousand feet. But here it was between four and five thousand feet. There was snow on the mountain tops. It had warmed up tremendously in an hour's time. I had unzipped my jacket coming back down the hill even though it was still cool. The exertion of the walk added to the warmth of the sun.

"Most people have no idea what they're seeing," she said, giving me a casual glance then looking back up the hill with the same intensity, I imagined, as when she had been looking at me wending my way down the hill towards her.

I thought of when I had been on the other side of the hill, how I had watched two ravens flying in the wide valley between two hills, the only trees on the hills little scrubby things. I thought how the valley formed a sort of amphitheater, their cawing was so clear. The thought crossed my mind that they liked how their voices sounded in that space and that's why they were flying there. Besides, it was a good place to rise and glide on the currents. Such a beautiful place, I thought, much more interested in the beauty of the place than in the petroglyphs. They had just been an excuse to go for a walk. On the top of the hill I had an excellent view of the sweeping landscape: far off in one direction the black smudge of ancient lava flows, and further off in the opposite direction the glittering of White Sands, miles upon miles of snow-white sand dunes. And seemingly nearest of all, the mountains crowned with snow, rising sharply above the semidesert land.

"Voices travel easily here," I said.

She nodded and gave a cautious glance in the direction of the young men with their fire and their loud radio.

"They spent the night," she said in a hushed voice. "They had that music going on all night, too. One of 'ems comes up to my RV and says, we gots extra ice. We's wondering if you wants it. And I could hear the other of 'em snickering off at a distance, one of 'em shouting something in Spanish. Don't think I don't know what he meant," she said giving me a meaningful eye. For the first time I noticed the RV in the parking area. I hadn't given it any thought up until then. I had seen it but hadn't thought about it. I suddenly realized that was her home. "My dogs was barking up a storm when he comes up to the RV in the middle of the night. I went to the door with my rifle. I've done used it many times in my life, and I pointed it at him and thanked him for offering the ice but told him I didn't need none. I told him to go back with his friends."

I looked at the two dogs that were tied up by her RV. I hadn't heard them bark. She noticed me looking at them. A saddened and pained expression came to her face.

"I can't even take 'em for a walk so they can relieve 'emselves. They won't use the restroom anywhere by the RV. And with 'em over there," she motioned with her head in the direction of the loud music, "I don't dare go too far from my RV and the rifle. It's everything I own in that RV." She motioned with her head towards her walking stick. "I can use this like a police baton if I need to. I've been trained how to use a police baton by my nephew who's a policeman in Roswell."

"It's sure beautiful here," I said. "It's a shame some people have to ruin it with such noise."

I stared in the direction of the young men's camp. Two cars and a truck parked in a semicircle. The blankets were still hanging from the ropes. The men were sitting around the fire. Every now and then one of them would get up to throw some wood on the fire. They were talking loud and sometimes laughing. It was time for breakfast, but they were drinking beer. No smell of bacon and eggs or coffee. They were speaking in Spanish but the meaning of the words was drowned out by the loud music.

"All night," she said, "they was playing that damn music all night, and drinking all night. I seen one of 'em drive off yesterday before it got dark and come back with two cases of beer. I knowed what they had on their minds last night. There I was all alone across the parking lot, but I showed that one the rifle. They knowed I would of used it."

It's true that when I walked down the hill I didn't want to talk with anyone. I was on vacation for a week, and my vacation was to get away from people. I saw too many people, talked to too many people, in my job as a Claims Representative with Social Security in Clovis. I hated that town, dull beyond belief. I had been there two years. I could see being there one more year tops. The short time I had been there more than half of the office staff had left. New people came and it wasn't long before they were ready to leave, especially if they were young. I thought of Jerry. He started working in the office a few months after I did. He was a year younger than me and had just finished a master's degree in history or something. He immediately hated Clovis. It took me about six months longer largely because before I got the job I was about as broke as you could be. For months I had only been eating one meal a day. I still felt a bit of amazement every time I went to the grocery store and realized I could buy anything I wanted to eat. Jerry had grown up in the mountains of northern New Mexico, and he still had family there. The plains of eastern New Mexico saddened him as did the fact that Clovis was only ten miles from the Texas border and in many ways *was* Texas, West Texas, culturally and linguistically. You had to go about a hundred miles before you got to anyplace bigger than Clovis and then you weren't anyplace too interesting. At times when I'd be getting back to Clovis from a trip and it'd be getting dark, I'd notice the lights of the farms, solitary lights at great distances from each other. Those lights seemed terribly lonely to me. And there were great stretches of plains, maybe thirty, forty, fifty miles where you wouldn't see a single light.

I think Jerry might have liked it in Clovis his first day. But that was it. He liked the fact that he had a Civil Service job and liked to talk about how tough the exams had been and how it surprised him when he saw what a high score he had gotten. He liked the idea of the security of a Civil Service job, and though he despised Clovis, he was determined to stick it out for a couple years until he got enough experience so that he could transfer somewhere else. He survived by going to a bar after work and having a few beers, and during the weekend he'd have more than a few beers. It wasn't long before he'd show up Monday mornings looking haggard. At first it was from too much drinking and then later it was from too much driving. The isolation of the place was getting to him. He called Clovis "Little Texas," which is what people from northern New Mexico call that eastern part of New Mexico stretching south to Hobbs. We got along well in the office, but outside of it we didn't have much to say. When he started driving back home to spend the weekends with his family, his father and mother, his attitude about Clovis grew better for a while. He would leave after work on Fridays and not return to Clovis until late Sunday night or early Monday morning. That's why he was looking so haggard. The drive was over 250 miles each way. But he preferred that to spending a long weekend in Clovis. Every weekend you stayed in Clovis was long. He'd go back home and hang out with an old friend or two or with a relative. Or he'd go fishing with his dad at a small lake not far from their ranch, a lake they usually had to themselves. Jerry especially liked fishing at night. I don't know if he ever caught anything. In the break room at work he'd talk about how he and his dad would sit in the rowboat with their lines in the water, and how peaceful it was, and how bright the night sky was so full of stars. He talked about the dark water and how it lapped against the boat, and sometimes it'd get real cold, but they had thick coats, and that was one of the best things he could think of in life, being in that boat with his father, gently buoyed by the water, whispering a few words to each other but mostly being quiet, breathing the fresh, thick smells brought by a breeze blowing over the lake at night.

So it was a great shock when I came into work one Monday morning and Marge told me Jerry was dead. It had happened Friday night. He was half way home when he collided into a truck that had pulled out onto the highway hauling a combine behind it. Jerry had been drunk. When Marge said that I recalled that Jerry had once told me that before he left town on Friday nights he'd stop for a six-pack to drink along the way. I hadn't thought anything of it. You'd get so bored driving across the plains for such long stretches that beer helped make the time pass faster. I had done it many times the first year I was in Clovis when I'd leave or come back. Leaving I'd drink beer to celebrate that I was getting away from Clovis for a while. Coming back, it was to deaden my senses, make me forget what I was coming back to. The last year I had been cutting back on the drinking, ever since I heard about Jerry.

The few friends I had in Clovis liked to go out dancing and drinking every weekend so it was impossible to completely stop drinking if I wanted any kind of social life. We especially liked going to dance halls out in the middle of nowhere, or so it seemed. It might be some old tin building in the middle of a cornfield or cotton field, but it would be packed with people. Most of them Mexican or Mexican American field workers who had come up from the valley of Texas or from across the border. You wouldn't hear any English spoken. It seemed like paradise after Clovis. Some nights we'd get so drunk we'd get lost on the dirt roads that radiate in every direction. And some nights we'd pull to the side of the road wherever we happened to be and pass out there. One morning we woke up and headed on our uncertain way and came to a small town called Earth. Earth, Texas. We thought it was hilarious. Towns on the plains had names like that, House, Weed, Muleshoe. Sometimes there'd be a sign with a name but no town. Just a few scattered farms.

When I came down from the hill, I didn't feel like talking with anyone. Five days a week I continually interviewed people and filled out form after form. We had a room at the office that was filled with different types of forms to be used depending on the claim being filed. Besides Social Security retirement, there were student benefits, death benefits, black lung, renal dialysis, and on and on. And we were also responsible for a whole separate program, Supplemental Security Income or SSI. It was a bureaucratic nightmare. Laws and regulations were continually being changed. As soon as you learned something, you'd find out it had been superseded by a new law or regulation. It was maddening. The best thing you could do was file away the continual new information in your regulation books and try to remember where it was when you encountered the situation. Each day would start out with a half hour of quiet time where you'd try to catch up on the work that had piled up from the day before, the days before, the weeks before. Cases in their manila folders would be piled high on your desk, but before you made much progress, the doors would be opened and the waiting area would be packed and the phones would be ringing. The look on Marge's face every time the doors were opened reflected the feelings everyone had: dread and despair. We were encouraged to put in overtime. That was the only way to keep up with the case load. Work became your life.

Even from as far away as I was on top of that hill, looking down at the parking area and seeing the small figure sitting at the picnic table, I could tell the person would want to talk. I scanned the terrain for another trail, but it was the only way back to my car. There was a fence as far as I could see and only one opening. She knew I would have to pass by her to get back to my car. So she waited patiently. There was no one else for her to talk with. Only the young men who had been drinking all night. Who she feared and loathed. She had turned her back to them, but she was alert, her dogs would bark if the men came towards her. She could use her stick to defend herself. She was trained in the use of a police baton.

"Noticed the lizard?"

"Lizard?"

"It's by what I call the centipede petroglyph. Though someone told me they thought it looked like a scorpion. It's like a pole ladder with a crescent on top. I have a photograph of it. I have a photograph of a good many of these pictographs. I mean petroglyphs. Some people use either word to mean petroglyphs. I don't think it's right though. Though I do slip once in a long while and say pictograph when I mean petroglyph. Pictographs are paintings you know. Usually red, black, yellow, white, those colors. And petroglyphs are carvings. Or what I call pecked art. A lot of 'em are just pecked away one little peck at a time. Especially in something like these basalt rocks." With a sweeping motion she circumscribed the hill. I looked up at the hill and thought of the petroglyphs I had seen up there. The only animal petroglyphs I remembered seeing were a few that looked like birds, and one that might have been a deer or an antelope, and a couple that looked like bighorn sheep because of the horns, though the bodies were highly stylized.

"I don't remember seeing a lizard though I saw a couple that looked like bighorn sheep."

"Yep," she said looking in the direction of her dogs, "there's several of 'em up there." She glanced in the direction of the young men with their radio blaring and their fire burning. All three were sitting around the fire. From time to time you'd hear a laugh or a loud word in Spanish. Though because of the music you couldn't make out the words. "They disgust me," she said, turning around to look at me. "I can't even take my poor dogs for a walk so they can relieve themselves. I can't do it as long as they're there partying. You see how those poor dogs are suffering?" She turned to look at her dogs again. I looked at them. They did seem to be suffering. They hadn't barked for a while, and their faces seemed worried. "They'd as soon burst as go this close to the RV. They won't dirty anywhere close to where they live."

She looked back at the hill. "You remember the position of the legs?"

"What?"

"The legs," she said, "on the bighorn sheep. If the legs look like they're running, it could mean there's good hunting of bighorn sheep in those mountains over there." She motioned with her head in the direction of the mountains behind her, the mountains topped with snow. "Of course there's no bighorn there now. But when some of those petroglyphs were done there were. Some of those petroglyphs are easily over a thousand years old. And somes are as new as when the Apaches were wandering through here a hundred years ago. Maybe a little longer. You know I seen a petroglyph in Utah I think it was of what I could have sworn was a mastodon. I didn't have a camera, but I done a little sketching of it, and I showed it to a park ranger, and he said he believed it was a mastodon though he had never seen a petroglyph of one. He said there hadn't been mastodons in that region for over 6,000 years. I told him generally where I seen it, and he said he was gonna go out looking for it first chance he had. I've long wondered if he ever found it. I don't get out to Utah anymore, not in many moons, just New Mexico and Texas. And mainly Texas down below El Paso all the way to the Big Bend. There's petroglyphs galore. And some pictographs too."

"So the way the legs are, that means something?" I reminded her. I was getting interested. When I looked at the petroglyphs on the hill I had wondered what possible meanings

108

there could be to them, but I thought that knowledge was something that was long lost. It intrigued me to think that this old lady could be a connection to that past.

"It's what I had wanted to tell you about the lizard. There's a petroglyph there of a lizard with three legs straight but one bent in the direction of White Sands. I think that was a sign meaning in that direction there's a water hole or a trail. And if a limb is missing that means something. Evenings I write what I've learned about these petroglyphs. Some of it I learned from talking to old Indians many years ago. I'd show them a photograph or a drawing, and they'd say smiling, "That's a rabbit dance." Sometimes they'd frown and not say anything. So I figured it was about their religion. Much of it they couldn't make heads or tails of. "That must be old," they'd say. Or they'd say, "I don't know what Indians done that." But there are all kinds of things they saw I'd never have guessed at. How it was information about water holes, and trails, and plentiful game. And, too, magic stuff and sometimes just funny stuff. Like Indian comic strips long before comics were invented."

She cast another glance in the direction of her dogs. When she looked back at the hill, there was a look of irritation on her face. The music from the radio continuing to blare.

Several times I tried to make excuses that I had to go on, but each time she cut me short. She talked about how she lived in the outdoors, that is, in her RV in the outdoors. When she wasn't working for the park service in New Mexico or Texas she'd work caretaking a ranch. Some people worried about her, she said, being a woman alone. But she had done it all these years and been fine. She knew how to take care of herself. She enjoyed the work, she said, and then frowned as she turned around to see the men at their fire, the radio blaring.

"I drove off early this morning and called the park service. Told them how these men were having a drinking party and who knows what else they were doing. But the park service don't care about that. They said it's public land and they can have a party if they want to. I told them how they've been making this fire by gathering the wood from around here. That's not allowed. They need to have brought their own wood.

But the ranger didn't seem to be too concerned about it. He don't have to hear that radio blaring all hours. He don't have them coming to his RV in the middle of the night asking if you want their extra ice. Ice! What a stupid thing to be asking in the middle of the night. I heard one of them by the fire saying they had something else for me too. I knows what's on their minds. I wasn't born yesterday. I know how to fire a gun. I've fired one plenty." She looked back in the direction of the men. I could see in her mind it was a test of wills between her and her dogs and them. They couldn't leave anytime too soon as far as she was concerned. She kept looking for signs that they were leaving or to see what else they were doing wrong that she could report to the park service.

"It is a shame," I said for the second or third time, "that people can't enjoy this place for what it is." She looked at me and nodded, a stern nod. "They have to bring their noise with them." I looked around at the whole sweep of the land, not a sign of a house or any building. I sort of envied her living out in such beauty.

"Generally, the people I meet out here are such fine people. They have interesting things to say and are full of questions about the petroglyphs. But those men over there, they haven't gone up in that hill once. They don't care about petroglyphs. This is just a party to 'em," she said contemptuously. "I don't have anything against Mexicans. I've known lots of good Mexicans. But these ones got the wrong notions. They wouldn't have a easy time with me. I think they know that. That's why they haven't been saying anything to me today. They saw that rifle last night." The look on her face was sheer defiance. The corruption of the world had invaded her peace of mind, her pristine land. But she wasn't dumb about the world, she had lived in it, understood its corruption, and she could withstand it. She had her stick, her gun, her dogs, and her determination. That's what I thought looking at the stern features of her face.

A fleeting thought went through my mind that I must have qualified as a good Mexican, otherwise she wouldn't have been talking to me the way she was. I thought of when I was a kid growing up in Las Vegas, New Mexico. When I was about eleven or twelve years old, I'd hang out at the Rough Riders' Museum in New Town. It was located near the Serf movie theater at that time. There was always some old man or old woman taking care of the place, and they loved nothing more than to talk for hours. That is, for them to talk and you to listen. I enjoyed listening to them, and it made me pause to think that some of them were my age before 1900! They were doors to the past, and they made that distant past seem real in ways books never could do.

All the people who worked at the museum were Anglos, and at the time I guess I didn't think a lot about it except that where I lived in Old Town across the river there were very few Anglos. But as soon as you crossed the river to New Town, Anglos were everywhere. I only remember being called a dirty Mexican once, so there wasn't prejudice that way. None that I encountered. It was more, "you live on your side of town, and we'll live on our side of town." But being a kid I didn't think too much about it one way or another. And I was always interested in the past, so I naturally gravitated to the Rough Riders' Museum. But when the old woman said "good Mexicans," I flashed back to that time in Las Vegas, and I suddenly thought, I bet when those old people at the museum saw me come though the door they thought, here's that nice little Mexican boy who likes to listen to our stories. Or Spanish boy. The word Spanish was used a lot instead of Mexican back then. Mexican had a demeaning connotation. When I listened to their stories, I didn't think of myself as Mexican or Spanish. I just thought of myself as a boy. Through their memories I'd find myself in the past seeing it through their eyes. After listening to them for a few hours I'd return home across the river. They were pleasant enough to me, but we were different. That's what I suddenly saw.

"I have a long way to go," I finally told her. It had almost been an hour since I had come down the hill and tried to sneak by her. I was glad now that I had listened to her, that I had come to know a little bit about her. The hill with its petroglyphs became more meaningful and so had this beautiful place. Before I had only seen it as a place, but now I saw it as a person. It was where she lived and worked until she moved on to be a caretaker of a ranch or went off to explore petroglyphs in Texas below El Paso. I realized she didn't know anything about me. I didn't have an opportunity to say much, and she didn't ask me any questions. She had plenty to say, and after the first few minutes when I felt imposed on, I found myself getting caught up in her story, her life spent in the outdoors, and her passion for petroglyphs. I thought about how she spent her evenings writing down notes about what she had learned about petroglyphs during a lifetime. I wondered if she'd ever publish a book, but I doubted it. She seemed to be in her early to mid seventies. It would be a big step to go from her note writing to writing a book. She didn't really say she wanted to write a book. She just said she wrote down notes.

Even with my telling her I had to go, she kept on talking. It took another fifteen minutes or so before I could get away. I told her I appreciated her telling me about the petroglyphs. She looked pleased hearing that. That was her job here. That's why she had waited patiently for me to make my hesitant way down the hill towards the only exit through the fence. She wore her park service hat and that made it her duty to accost strangers. Nothing personal. It was about getting information to the public. But it was personal, and I was glad to have gotten to know about her life. And I was glad she didn't want to know about my life. That kept it from getting too personal. She could keep reverting back to petroglyphs and that kept it on a public servant to public level.

Before I left she handed me a brochure about the petroglyphs. That clinched it, made it a professional talk. I thanked her and went over to my car. As I drove out of the parking area I looked at the three men sitting around their fire. They watched me leave. My closed windows made their blaring radio sound tolerable. I drove on to the gravel road and headed to the highway several miles away. I looked back and saw the smoke from the fire. I couldn't see the old woman, though I was certain she had remained where I left her, sitting on the concrete bench. The blaring radio was probably sounding louder to her now that I was gone. Her thoughts must have returned to her patiently suffering dogs who hadn't relieved themselves in two days. I imagined not too many people came to see the petroglyphs this time of the year. I found myself worrying about her. Worrying that no one else would come that day to see the petroglyphs. She'd be sitting in that beautiful country, but really she'd love to be talking to someone. Not that she hated her solitude. But she got enough of that I was sure when she worked as a caretaker. Also, it was her duty to talk to people at the park, inform them about the petroglyphs—she had her official hat.

I thought, she'll be alright. I thought of the three rough looking men. They didn't look like they were planning on leaving that day. It was Saturday, and they probably were going to spend another night drinking beer or whatever else, what the old woman had hinted at, that there was something else going on there, not just beer drinking. I wondered what she meant by that or if she fully knew—maybe just a suspicion she had. I tried to imagine what it would be like for her that coming night. Lights turned off early in her RV, and if she went to bed it would be with her clothes on and her rifle by her side. But probably she wouldn't go to bed until early in the morning. Until she had not heard a sound for hours. She'd probably pull up a chair to the side of a window and peer out the edge of a curtain, looking in the direction of the men and their fire. Listening for her dogs to sound the alarm that a dark shape was moving towards the RV. She'd strain her eyes to see any movement, all the while worrying about the safety of her dogs. And what if like the night before one of them came stumbling towards the RV, slurring his words, yelling out to her to open her door? What excuse would he use this time to get her to come out? Surely he wouldn't use that stupid reason again, did she want their extra ice. What a dumb thing to be trying to give someone late at night—to a woman alone. And she'd probably think about what one of the other two men by the fire had shouted not so much to her but at her. It was clear to her what he meant even though he said it in Spanish. She had experienced all kinds of men in her long life, and she knew what certain expressions meant just by the intonation of the voice, it didn't matter what language was spoken. She understood she wasn't too old to be considered of sexual interest to men who were drinking all day and night and taking who knows what other drugs.

I looked about at the land I was passing through, and I thought, this is a severe land. I thought about how at ease she had been in this land for so many years. I thought of how when she took care of ranches, how she'd be the only person for many miles. She knew when the dogs barked it was probably because of coyotes or some other animal. That didn't worry her. But these human animals did. They were frightful enigmas. First they were men, and young, and in her eyes lustful. And their speaking Spanish made her wonder what they might be saying about her. The Spanish made them seem foreign; there was something threatening about it. Even though she had heard Spanish spoken much of her life, usually in the background. She didn't give any indication that she understood Spanish. All this combined with their drinking, their noisiness, the blaring radio, the fact that her dogs couldn't relieve themselves because she couldn't take them for a walk as long as they were there, all this must have made her dread the coming night. And I thought, she's an old woman alone with her RV in a remote and lonely part of the country. She could shoot her rifle, every bullet, and no one would hear her that night. I thought, it wouldn't happen. She wouldn't be shooting out into the dark, frozen with fear, hitting nothing in the darkness. I thought, it won't happen that night. But it worried me, nevertheless, thinking it could happen.

I worried about her. And as I looked out at the land about me, it was a land totally transformed from the land I had driven through when I came here. It was still an austerely beautiful land, but now it had the element of this woman's drama. This land was now her; it was human; it had its human history. There were the petroglyphs, a record of centuries, and the old woman whose passion it was to study them. She had made the petroglyphs come to life for me seeing them through her eyes. I had climbed the hill and dutifully looked at a number of them, but I understood so little about the petroglyphs—before she explained what she knew about them—that the human history behind them escaped me at the time. I found myself more caught up in the invigorating feel of an early morning walk in early winter, the exertion of climbing the hill, having to watch my step on the eroded trail, and feeling the faint warmth of the rising sun above a mountain capped with snow, the snow thousands of feet higher in elevation. But it was also a land with its fears over the presence of three men who had spent a night drinking beer and sitting around a fire in the morning, drinking their first beer of the day, beer ice cold from how cold it had gotten that night. I brooded thinking about her worrying about the three men. Her worrying about their seeming harshness, the potential of sexual violence. And I thought, there's no reason for her to fear them just because they speak Spanish. But I knew her fears went way beyond that. She could see I was from the same background as they were. But I hadn't spent the whole night drinking and being loud a couple hundred feet from her RV—and there was also their blaring radio. I had gone up the hill to where the petroglyphs were. We held that in common. The men had been there a whole day and none of them had gone in the direction of the hill to see the petroglyphs. They only went as far as they had to go to gather wood for their fire. She had said this as if it were a slighting offense. How could she relate to them if they had no interest in the petroglyphs? I thought of what I had read in the newspaper the day before. In a city just a hundred miles away a man had cut off another man's head and had also cut out the heart and thrown it in a neighbor's yard. When the police came he claimed they'd never find the heart because he had eaten it. And I thought how in El Paso a man was coming to trial accused of murdering women over a period of years and burying their bodies in shallow graves in the desert. I thought of how common it was to turn on the Albuquerque news and hear of yet another dead body found someplace, often women. And I thought of the single mother murdered in her own home with a butter knife.

I thought, the old woman will be alright, her fears are unfounded. But as quickly I thought, maybe not. Men drinking for two days straight, out in the middle of nowhere. I had already put many miles between her and me. The further I got away from her, the more I focused on what she had said, that she could take care of herself. I thought of her walking stick that she said she could use like a police baton. I thought of her dogs and of her rifle. I thought of the many years she had lived alone as a caretaker of ranches. And I began feeling more confident that she would be alright. What else could I think? I had only known her for a little over an hour. A brief stop on my way back to a city and job I hated. An early morning walk up a hill covered with jumbled black stones, many of them with petroglyphs. An early morning walk in the icy air of a land not desert but verging on it. A land grimly and desolately beautiful in the morning shadows cast by the scrub and rocks and little hills. The mountains towering. The land sweeping away towards the lower elevation of White Sands and down to the deserts of Mexico. A cold early morning walk far from people is what I had expected.

✧ A Good Night For Traveling

I cut off his ear. It surprised him. It surprised me. I had never done anything like that before.

I was practically out the door before I heard him screaming: MY EAR, HE CUT OFF MY FUCKING EAR! Not really, I thought, as the door closed behind me. It was only the earlobe. I still held it in my hand. I threw it underneath a parked car and folded up my knife, a slim titanium knife from Germany that disappeared into my pocket. There were two men immediately outside the Cabaret. They looked at me and quickly looked away when they saw the knife. When the door closed behind me, you couldn't hear the guy yelling about his ear. The Cabaret was in a small strip mall that had totally different businesses from what it must have had when it was originally built. I walked briskly past a laundromat that was squeezed between the topless Cabaret and an adult bookstore. My car was parked at the far end of the strip mall. I got to my car and looked back before getting in. I had expected a crowd to be coming after me, but no one, not the security guard from the Cabaret, not even the guy with his bleeding ear. I got in the car wondering if it'd start. Things have gone wrong in my life before so I always wonder. But that night the car started without a problem. I pulled out into the traffic of Missouri Avenue with my lights off. I didn't realize it until I had gone several blocks. I turned on the lights and thought about how great it was that I didn't turn the lights on. It would have been hard for anyone to get my license plate number. I had only gone a little over a mile when I heard the sound and felt the movement that I've come to understand is a flat tire nine times out of ten. I pulled off into a dark side street.

I'm a great believer in synchronicity: things happen in the most unexpectedly connected ways. My cutting off his earlobe and my getting the flat tire, they were inevitable.

I never thought I'd land up in El Paso. Tucson is where I had always wanted to move. Joyce wrote to me from the hinterlands of Minnesota asking why I had moved to the edge of the world, and she hinted that maybe Tucson would be a good place for us. When we lived in Amarillo (not together), I must have told her a hundred times that I was going to move to Tucson someday. And it was something I really believed even though I had never been to Tucson—and still haven't. I haven't given up on the idea of moving to Tucson. Someday.

I forget the name of the city in Minnesota where she lived. It was a funny sounding name. She went there to finish a Master's degree she had started years back. We wrote for the first year. Now it's been a couple years since we've written. I forget whose turn it was to write. We were friends of sorts in Amarillo. She was living with a friend of mine—I was going to say a good friend but I caught myself. I've never had a good friend. When they broke up, she and I stayed friends of sorts. He moved away, and she and I went out dancing and drinking, but it was never anything intimate. Though once we did share a bed for a night, but I had a bad cold, and she refused to take off her clothes, though finally she did take off her top and bra and let me touch and fondle her breasts. I'll never forget her saying, "There's no milk in them." She had a baby girl. I had never sucked a woman's breast that had milk. That is, not since I was a baby, and I certainly didn't remember anything about that. Her saying that about her milk startled me; that and the rigid way she held her body and the roughness of her jeans made me

118

lose any interest in sex I might have had. But now I'm thinking, one of these days I'll have to try that, a woman whose breasts are ripe with milk. Pump it out with my lips. But I don't want to have kids. That's a complication.

I wrote back to her and said, "I guess in a way you can say El Paso is at the end of the world, or at the edge of this country, just across the river is Mexico." It took me months to cross the bridge. I didn't write that to her. I'm just saying it. It seemed like I was always busy the first few months I was in El Paso. First finding an apartment and a job. Then learning the job. Then learning parts of El Paso. Parts of El Paso seemed enough like Mexico that I didn't feel any hurry to cross the bridge to Juárez. And when I finally went across, I spent two hours wandering around, and that was enough for me. Border towns don't have much to recommend them. I've never had a desire to go back. Besides, in El Paso there's great Mexican food, and you can speak Spanish. Juárez is almost always in view, so close, just across the river. Parts of it you see sprawling away into the desert. But I don't have any curiosity about it.

She only mentioned Tucson in one letter. I don't remember what I wrote in response. Probably nothing too encouraging. I wasn't ready to move to Tucson yet. I felt committed to El Paso for at least three years. Pay off my car, pay off bills, then I could move on.

I had a vivid dream about Joyce shortly after I moved to El Paso. I had flown up to see her in Minnesota. In the dream she had three children though she really only has one. I took her and her three children out to eat at a fancy place a few miles outside of the city she lived in. During the meal she asked me if I'd adopt her three children because they weren't adjusting well to her lifestyle. "What lifestyle is that?" I asked her. What she said was ambiguous. It left me feeling uncomfortable. In the dream I was tempted to say yes that I'd adopt her children. But the more I thought of it, the less I liked the idea. I thought of how small my apartment was in El Paso. In my dream I thought of it being much smaller than it was. And then she dropped her kids off at her place and she drove me to the airport. When we arrived at the airport it was snowing lightly. She walked with me to the boarding gate. I looked out the window and it was snowing real hard. "It's not a good night for traveling," I told her. She didn't say anything. She hadn't said anything since I had told her at the restaurant that I couldn't adopt her children. I was standing next to her, but the look on her face said, you are already on the plane, and the plane is far away. All the times we had gone dancing in Amarillo, all the good times we had had, I had never tried to kiss her. And so I kissed her thinking of all the times we had danced, of the times we had held each other tight, of all the times we had laughed. Her face turned into a blizzard at the approach of my lips. My lips touching her lips felt stung as if her lips had turned to chollas, to cactus spines. Her eyes bore into me with the coldness of the dark side of the moon. She didn't say a word, but as I boarded the plane it seemed to me she had said, "I hope your plane crashes in the snowy fields of Iowa."

Two days after cutting off his earlobe I felt bad about it. The night I did it I had mixed feelings. Mainly, I think, because of the flat tire I had minutes later fleeing the scene. When I pulled off to the dark side street and heard the siren, I thought they were after me. But I stayed there parked for a long time with my car lights off thinking of my flat tire, and I didn't hear another siren. And I slowly began to realize that when I heard the siren, it was too early for it to have been someone after me. I had only left the Cabaret a few minutes earlier. I reminded myself how El Paso was a large city with its share of crime, and surely sirens must be going off all the time depending on the part of the city. I thought of that and my flat tire and how dark it was outside. And I thought about the earlobe I had cut with my titanium knife from Germany that I had bought for fifty dollars on sale. I hadn't wanted to spend that much on a pocketknife, but it was the slimmest pocketknife I had seen. I liked that it'd disappear in my pocket. I had never cut anything with it until I cut the earlobe. How easy it was, I thought, sitting in my car in the dark.

It was past three when I got home that night. It was past one when I left the Cabaret. And it must have been almost an hour before I got out of the car to change the tire. It was almost as if I was waiting for the police to pick me up, but when they didn't, I went on with the business at hand. Because of the previous three flat tires during the past year I had bought a flashlight to keep in the glove compartment. The last flat tire had happened a short time before it had gotten dark. I was returning to El Paso from Albuquerque and had pulled off onto a side road and driven fifteen miles to investigate an out-of-the-way town whose name intrigued me. But as is usually the case, there was nothing to the town beyond its name. It was a small cluster of adobe houses, a number of them in ruin, and a few trailers. No stores of any kind, not even a gas station. I had driven a little beyond the end of town, running out of town before I realized it. I then pulled off to the side of the road and turned around. I turned around on a hill above the town. I could see the entire sad cluster of houses and trailers. I said the name of the town to myself several times as if it were a magical incantation that could transform the dusty town before me to a town of my imagination, the town its name had invoked in my mind.

As I drove back through the town I heard the sound and felt the movement that made me pull off the road at the first open space. It was a small parking area in front of a trailer that was the town's post office. It was closed and the parking area was empty. I'm downtown, I thought, trying to lighten my spirits. I thought how it was the third flat tire since I bought the tires in December. That was as many flat tires as I had had the previous ten years. I shivered at the thought that another half hour and it would have been dark, and I might have been stuck in that town for the night. The whole time I was changing the tire I only saw one car go by. I didn't see anyone walking around, didn't even see anyone peering out a window.

So a few days later I bought a flashlight. And a month later I was thankful I had it in the car. Otherwise, I would have had to leave the car there. It took what seemed like a terribly long time to change the tire. Things weren't progressing very fast until I propped the flashlight on some rocks to free that hand. I got home and washed up a little. I went to bed, but I still felt extremely grimy. It was a hot night, and I had sweated as I changed the tire. I tried to sleep but I couldn't. Finally, I got up and took a shower. As I showered, I could feel the night washing away from me. It had entangled itself in the hair on my head, in the hair in my nostrils, in my armpits, in my pubic hair. And it all washed away with the help of shampoo. The water seemed to even soak through my skull and clean out my brain.

I went to bed and tossed about for a while, more upset about the flat tire than anything, wondering if it was just my bad luck or if someone could be behind it. I wondered who it could be, but it didn't make sense. Just my bad luck, I thought, as I fell asleep.

And that night I had only the second dream I've ever had of Joyce. It was snowing, and I was kissing her. But it was like I was kissing the falling snow. And while there was plenty of light when I started kissing her, when my lips left her lips, it immediately grew dark. I thought to myself, Joyce is the darkest night of the coldest winter. And I turned away from her not expecting her to say good-bye, and I was right; I didn't hear her say a word. Then I got in my car and drove away. I headed into the plains. Almost two hundred miles away was the small city that was my home. A place I loathed. The further I drove, the heavier the snow became until it was snowing so hard that I couldn't see the road in front of me. I drove slow and opened the car door to see the road. It's a blizzard, I thought. And I thought of Joyce and how she could have asked me to spend the night on her sofa. She knew how far I had to drive; she saw it was snowing. But she was through with me. The kiss had done that. It had brought the snow, the cold, the blizzard. And I thought, I might die out here in the plains if the car goes off the road; I could freeze. Joyce wouldn't care, I thought. She would think I deserved it. It was funny to have a dream of snow and cold when it was such a hot summer night.

Things can deteriorate so fast. I'm thinking of the evening news I watched the night after I had the flat tire. I had gotten home about three in the morning, but I was too wound up to sleep. I had tried. I had gone to bed after washing my hands and arms, which were filthy from changing the tire, but an hour later I was wide awake. I had spent the whole hour thinking of the damn flat tire and wondering if it was a conspiracy. The whole time I hadn't given a thought to the Cabaret or to the man whose earlobe I had cut off. But once I thought about it, I realized I should have taken a shower. I got out of bed and took a long shower.

I probably didn't fall asleep until after five, and when I woke up it was late in the afternoon. I scrambled some eggs and watched TV until the evening news. I hadn't expected that what I had done would be the lead story, and I was right. The lead story was what got me thinking about how things can deteriorate so quickly. A young man was celebrating his birthday and ran out of money, so he robbed a convenience store—well named for robbers—took beer and maybe thirty or forty dollars from the cash register. And to make a bad situation worse, he stabbed the clerk in the neck. They showed a newsclip of the woman being taken out of the store on a stretcher. And then they said the young man had been caught and was trying to raise a $100,000 bond to get out of jail. I wondered what size bond would be placed on me if I landed in jail.

The next news story was about a car jacking. A young man driving home from work stops to get gas. He gets out of his truck and starts pumping the gas. A man he's never seen before comes up to him and shoots him in the stomach. Not a word was exchanged the whole time. A few hours later they find the truck crashed someplace in the city. The young man's in the hospital in critical condition.

Then followed the story of the arrest of an extended family in Deming for selling drugs and money laundering. More than twenty people had been arrested with more expected. A detective was interviewed who said they were making more money a year than the El Paso electric company. The reporter asked, "What's this about filthy money?" "That's right," said the detective, "that's probably what was the start of their downfall." "How's that?" the reporter's voice said. The camera stayed focused on the detective. "The money had a smell to it," he said, "that could permeate a whole building." The camera turned to the reporter. There was a perplexed look on her face. "How's that?" she said momentarily forgetting her professional demeanor. "The money stunk," the detective said, "because they buried their money in covered buckets or barrels. And they must have used a bucket or barrel that had had something awful in it at one time and still had residue, that's what I'm thinking. So for a period of a couple months there, all this filthy money is showing up around town. Merchants almost hate to take it, it looks and smells so bad. A well driller was paid two thousand cash in twenty dollar bills and the wife says the house stank for days. I hear one of the family members put her money in the washing machine before she spent it. I guess they all should have done that. But I'm glad they didn't. They'd probably still be out there today bringing in more drugs from Mexico." "I guess that's where the money laundering charge comes in?" the reporter said in an attempt to make a joke. But the detective was too humorless for that. He just gave her a blank look.

The weather came on and there hadn't been any mention about the Cabaret. I began switching between news stations. They were doing reports the other station had already done. I switched back to the first news station, watched the end of the weather report, watched the sports, and then the news anchors came back on for a last few minutes of news. "This is kinda strange," the male news anchor said, "the police are calling it the van Gogh assault. Late last night in a local cabaret, an altercation took place and a man cut off another man's earlobe. The police are looking for a Hispanic male about 5'10" tall. He's about 170 pounds, clean shaven, and with short hair." "Earlobe?" the female anchor grinned. "That's what the report says," the first anchor said staring at the paper in front of him. He looked up at the camera, and you could see he was trying hard to keep from grinning. "That's it for tonight," he said, and I turned off the television.

I had been feeling bad after the first news reports and thinking how things can deteriorate so fast. And then thinking about the $100,000 bail. But then seeing how they had placed my story last, and seeing how they had made light of it, and how they only had a general description of me that wasn't accurate, I began feeling better. I found myself chuckling about the news report about the van Gogh assault as if it hadn't happened in my life. What a stupid thing to have happened, I thought.

And I thought of the flat tire, and I thought of Joyce, and I thought of the Cabaret and the woman who was sitting at my table. I had bought her a drink, and my arm was around her bare shoulders. And then a large man came to our table and demanded that she get him a beer. She tried to get up, but I held her down with my arm. Before he had come up to our table, I had been thinking how she was slender like Joyce with the same sort of small breasts and how she laughed the same way and had a way of averting her eyes like Joyce. "There are plenty of waitresses here," I told him. He had lunged at me, but there was the table between us. I pushed the table against him as I stood up. That put him off balance plus who knows how much he already had had to drink. I didn't even remember taking the knife out of my pocket and opening it. It was a reflex. I went around the table, and he came back at me. I don't know why I cut off his earlobe. I guess it was because it was either that or stick it in his stomach or cut his throat and that could have killed him. Fortunately, I was sober enough to realize it wasn't worth killing a jerk like him. Joyce screamed, I mean the woman we were fighting over screamed, and I left. The flat tire was inevitable. But that was the worst of it. Here it was the next night, and it looked like nothing in my life would be changed. I thought of Joyce, and how it was over between us what never really was. Spilt blood ends it, I thought, thinking of the dancer at the Cabaret who I had bought a drink for. I could still feel my arm draped lightly over her bare shoulder. And I could still hear her laughter, which was almost a muffled laugh directed downwards. So much like Joyce. And then I realized I'd be going back to the Cabaret as soon as I'd grown a beard and my hair had grown longer.

Paclita ✧

1

When I'm standing outside my store and Paclita goes by, she doesn't look at me. She keeps her eyes straight ahead, but she can't help noticing me. I'm always looking right at her. But that's as bold as I get. Though once she did give me a quick glance over her slender shoulder. I felt embarrassed and quickly looked away. And for hours afterwards I was shaken up. Imagine if we had spoken.

My friends say they envy me because I'm single. Their wives have gotten fat, and their children are brats. They encourage me to make up lies, to tell them about impossible amorous conquests. I go along with it. It's amusing up to a point. I'm not handsome, but all my friends pretend that women couldn't help but find me irresistible. The truth is the only women I go to bed with are the women I have to pay. I'm a man's man. It's easy talking to a man, but a woman, I don't know where to begin. Except when they're customers; then I can be charming, or anyway I think I am. Customers don't care that I'm overweight, that my hair is thinning, that I look ten years older than I am, and that I'm not handsome. And with women who are customers, I even find myself from time to time telling a little joke. I'm always amazed and thankful that I can get them to smile. But in any other situation with women, I freeze. I can never think of what to say to break the ice. And I'm always thinking that women are finding faults with my looks and with my clothes not to say anything about my behavior.

I can't talk to any of my friends about Paclita. I'm afraid they might think she's much too young for me. But maybe that's just my concern. Certainly they wouldn't understand how petrified I become when I think of even saying a single word to her. And it's not as if I don't have ample opportunities to talk to her. She passes by my store most days. I can easily imagine what they'd say, "She must be in love with you, going by your store all the time. What more do you want? Do you want her to propose to you?" I can hear their disparaging laughter. But what they'd really say would probably be something much worse. If I didn't make my move, or if I did and she didn't have any interest in me, how would I be able to hold up my head around my friends? Me, the lady's man. My friends' wives would love it. They hate me because their husbands spend so much time hanging out at my store. My embarrassment would give them plenty to gossip about. "That Romeo Chits is no Romeo at all," they'd laugh. "All these outrageous stories our husbands have been telling us about his amorous conquests, and he can't even say hello to a girl, not a woman mind you, but just a girl. We've known it all along. All you have to do is take one look. What woman in her right mind would want him?" They'd find it all such a scream. Everyone would be laughing behind my back. I'd have to leave town.

2

I sleep in the small room at the back of my store. It seems sometimes that I spend my whole life in this store. That's why when I close up at midnight, I have to go someplace to eat. It's not that I'm always hungry; there are plenty of street vendors selling food within smelling distance of my front door. During the day I run up to one of them, grab something that's been attracting me with its scent, and take it back to the store. But when I close up at night, I can't wait to get out of the store, and at midnight, the only places open are a few restaurants and the bars. Since my drinking days are over—it bothers my stomach among other things—I land up in a restaurant. With the tourists, you have to stay open late. Sometimes sales don't start picking up until eight or nine at night. And when you get tourists who've had a little to drink, they might buy anything.

Friends are always hanging out at my store after they get off work. For them, work can be an hour here, an hour there, wherever they can see an opportunity to make some money. During the day they come and go. Some of them like to talk; others hardly say a word. I don't mind them. They all know to get out of the way when a tourist comes in the store. I always have a big bottle of mescal in the store so they can pour themselves a little drink. Sometimes they get drunk. I don't approve of it, but what can I say? They're my friends after all.

Me, I mostly drink tea I make on a hot plate. No wonder I can hardly sleep with so much caffeine in me. Even though I go to bed late, I'm always up before the sun rises. It's not that I have to get up so early. I don't open my store until eleven. True, I get to do some running around restocking items I've sold. But I could get it all delivered. I guess I just can't wait to get out of my store. I spend so many hours there as it is, my store and home, that I can't wait to wake up and rush out the door. Sometimes I just wander around. It's nice in the early morning. Nothing like the packed madness of the nights. It's another city. But the truth is, I just can't sleep that much. Even without all the caffeine in my system, it wouldn't be any different. I think my metabolism must just naturally make caffeine. It hardly ever seems that I have my eyes closed for more than an hour or two and then I'm fully awake.

A friend once told me that I live to go out to eat. He's one of the friends who usually joins me when I close after midnight

When he said that, I thought, if that's what he wants to believe, that's fine with me. But it's like I said, after a long day in the store, I just can't wait to get out of there. And I never look forward to getting back there to sleep. What I need is a separate place to live. But there are always friends in my store when I close up. What can I do, chase them away? Of course I have to invite them to go eat with me. And of course they're always short of money, the wife has it all, the children are eating it all. So, I treat. That's where all my profits go. That and a big bottle of mescal for my friends. With friends like these, you never get ahead. And they love you for it.

I go out to the cheapest place. I couldn't afford any place else, especially with three to six hungry mouths trailing after me. And the place we go to doesn't serve liquor, fortunately. Again, that's another reason I chose it. I'd be in the poorhouse if I started buying my friends drinks. I see it with the mescal. They don't think anything of having two, three, or four little glasses. If they could see what my eyes are saying to them, they'd stop after one or two little glasses. The bottle of mescal was a bad idea. Once, I hid the bottle. But all my friends did was complain how miserable they were, how ugly their wives were, what juvenile delinquents their children were. And on and on and on. I couldn't stand it. By ten that night, I pretended like I had accidentally found a bottle of mescal. "Look at this," I said, "Can you believe it? A great big bottle of mescal under this counter in the far corner. How did it get there?" My friends didn't care how it got there. They were just glad to see it returned to its rightful place where they could easily reach out and pour themselves a drink. That night they drank it like water. And were they ever drunk. That was the beginning of the threatening letters I get from their wives. Like I tell them when they come in my store to scream at me, "I don't force them to drink. I try to set an example by not drinking alcohol myself. Maybe a few sips, but that's it. They're grown men. If they don't drink here, they're going to drink someplace else. Do you want them in the bars where they can get in fights and end up cut up?" This makes them pause and think. But they still hate me. It's not my fault that their husbands prefer to spend moretime in my place than at their homes. Can their homes be that miserable a place?

So many times I want to talk with someone, anyone, about Paclita. Anymore, she's the foremost thought on my mind. If I was a drinking man, I probably would already have blabbered everything out. And the illusion we've created, my friends and I, of a swinging life would be shattered. What a ridiculous game this is, pretending that I'm a lady's man, that if they only were single, they'd have different women every night. They joke when we part at the restaurant at almost two in the morning, "Give her a good one." Sure, give her, give who a good one? There aren't any women. I don't even laugh at their jokes anymore. I have to force a smile. Sure, that's how it is. Sure. Sure. So I go home alone, to my store and home, alone with my thoughts of Paclita.

It amazes me that none of my friends ever point out Paclita. Isn't she beautiful? She passes by the store every day, and all of my friends have been outside my store at one time or another when she's gone by. And even though they're constantly casting longing glances after any woman younger than their grandmothers and older than their children, they've never seemed to notice Paclita. It's a mystery to me. It's not that I want them to say obscene things about her, but I'd like to think they find her attractive. But nothing. They don't even turn their heads. It's as if she didn't even go by. How can I tell them I'm in love with this girl, this nobody in their eyes? And how would I be able to explain that I can't even bring myself to speak to her! They'd find me a pitiful case indeed.

And so I don't talk to any of my friends about Paclita even though she's always on my mind. I wouldn't even know her name if a few months ago I hadn't noticed her talking to a small boy who was selling something by the curb. The way she smiled at him, it seemed like she knew him. After she left, I went up to him and asked him who she was.

"Who?" he said. I pointed to the receding figure, the exquisite figure, of Paclita. "Do you mean my cousin, Paclita?" I nodded yes.

"What do you want with her?" he said getting suspicious. By this time several of his little friends had gathered around us to see what was going on.

"Nothing," I said, "nothing," and went back into my store. What could I say? That I was in love with her? I panicked. I could have gotten some information out of him if I had been smart. If need be, I could have offered him money. He wouldn't have refused that. He would have told me everything I wanted to know. But I panicked that the truth would come out. I was afraid it was clearly written on my face, my love for Paclita. With a bunch of kids like that, the word would be out in no time. I'd be the laughingstock of Culebras. The word would get to Paclita that a fat, old man was in love with her. Would she turn into my door the next time she went by solely to spit on my floor? What if she said, "That's what I think of your love." That'd devastate me and leave my heart shattered like a city after an earthquake.

Before I fell in love with Paclita, I never felt self-conscious about the way I dressed. Now I feel embarrassed about the cheapness of my clothes, and I worry about how worn my shoes are. What if Paclita took a good look at me? What would she see?

One problem with going out to eat every night is that I've been gaining weight. And since I'm always treating my friends, I don't have any money left to spend on myself. I hate to look in mirrors and see how fat I've become. What would happen if some night after closing the store, I told my friends I was going to bed? What would they think? It'd be like with the bottle of mescal. They'd be miserable. And then with time they'd probably hate me. And there I'd be in fancy clothes, without Paclita, without friends. Where would I be then?

3

Today Paclita wore a large red ribbon in her braided hair. So simple and yet my breath was taken away. She gave me the longest look she's given me yet, and there I was gasping for air,

131

looking very stupid. There was a chance to speak to her, and I couldn't breathe!

I should have said, "What a beautiful ribbon but not anywhere as beautiful as you." Or at least I should have said, "What a beautiful ribbon."

Maybe she would have blushed, and maybe she would have said, "I only bought it yesterday. Red is my favorite color. Is red your favorite color too?"

There is a chance she would have said something like that, and I probably would have said, "Yes, yes, red is my favorite color. Especially when you wear it. You make red look more beautiful than I've ever seen red look. When I first saw the ribbon in your hair, I thought of some rare tropical flower."

And then what would she have said to that? Might she have said, "It's amazing the effect a simple ribbon can have." No, that doesn't sound right. Maybe she would have said, "When I wear red, it's because I'm thinking of the heart. And when I think of the heart, I think of love." No, no, that doesn't sound right at all. It's frustrating. I can imagine what she might say up to a point. And then it falls apart. It doesn't sound like a natural conversation. It sounds all made up, which it is. But I can imagine her though, lowering her eyes demurely and whispering something.

"I'm sorry," I would say, "I didn't hear what you said." I can see her raising her head and speaking boldly, much more boldly than I could ever do.

"Is it my imagination, or are you in love with me?"

That's all that needs to be said to make me deliriously happy.

"You're not imagining!" I would shout. "I *am* in love with you. Ever since you first went by my store. I thought even then I had to marry you. I thought you were the most beautiful woman in the world, and nothing has changed."

What if she frowned? What if confusion filled her face? What if she looked at me with horror and disgust? What if she turned and walked away, never to be seen again?

4

It seems like my friends' wives are coming into the store all the time. When they catch their husbands here, they lead them home. Sometimes the husbands refuse to budge, but then I don't see them for several days. If their husbands aren't in the store, they demand to know where they are.

"What whore is he with? Tell me."

"How do I know where he is?" I tell them. "I assume he's working to keep . . . ," but they don't let me finish.

"You're ruining our marriage," they say. Or, "Our children are growing up without a father because of you."

"They're grown men," I say. "I don't twist their arms to . . . ," but they cut me off.

"He comes home smelling of cheap perfume. He says you do it, why can't he."

"What are you talking about?" I say. "Cheap perfume? What does . . . ," again they don't let me finish.

"I know he's seeing other women, that bastard, and there I'm stuck with crying babies and children who won't behave because there's never a father around to discipline them."

"I sympathize," I tell them. "I don't encourage your husbands to . . . ," they never let me finish.

"You keep leading our men astray this way, Chits, and all the women of Culebras are going to revolt." Usually this is said when there are at least three wives in the store. "You're going to get yours, Chits," another woman will say. "You'll regret it," some other woman will add. If looks could kill, I long ago would have been buried.

I don't enjoy any of this. I wish it didn't have to happen. But even still the men keep coming even though every week or so their wives drag them away. I'm surprised no one's gotten divorced yet. But come closing time, there are always plenty of hungry friends hanging around to eat up my profits for the day.

From time to time, a wife will send her brother or cousin or uncle to come over and threaten me. But after a little talk and a little glass of mescal, they get friendly and stay until closing time. And of course I invite them to go out to eat. They become regulars, and then their wives start coming into the store to complain to me. It really takes a lot out of me always having to stand up to their assaults. If this is what marriage is about, forget it, I keep thinking to myself.

But then I can't get Paclita off my mind. Today, as I was standing outside my store talking to a friend, I saw Paclita approaching. As Paclita was about to pass us, I made like my friend had pushed me into her. It was the first time I had ever touched her, but I'm afraid I bumped into her too hard, stepping on her foot, because she cried out in pain.

"You stupid . . . ," she started to say and then dropped it. It was the first time we had ever looked at each other so directly, eye to eye.

"Why did you do this?" I turned and yelled at my friend.

"Do what?" he said, totally confused by what was going on.

"Pushing me into this . . . ," I had been looking at my friend and when I turned to look at Paclita she was gone. She was already half a block away, limping very fast.

"What's this about?" my friend said. "Do what? What did I do?"

"Forget it. It's not important." I lied. It had been the most important moment of my relationship with Paclita. My body had touched hers, and if she hadn't left so quickly, I would actually have spoken to her. What I had hoped would be a moment of triumph turned into a catastrophe. She called me "stupid" and might have called me something worse if she hadn't caught herself. What if I had said her name? I should have called after her, "Paclita, come back."

After this unfortunate experience I didn't see Paclita go by my store for almost two weeks. I was starting to despair that I would never see her again. But when I finally saw her go by again, I was talking with a customer, and in the middle of a sentence, I ran to the door and saw the back of Paclita. That blessed back! It was like I had seen a miracle. An angel, she seemed to me like an angel.

Some days it's hard to do business with my friends' wives there screaming at me, blaming me for everything that's going wrong in their lives. If a child gets a toothache I'm to blame. If a plate slips out of their hands when they're washing it, I'm the one they curse. If their husbands snore, it's my fault. And while they're letting me have it, their husbands sneak out and come back when their wives are gone. I don't enjoy this, not at all. It's bad for business, bad for my nerves, and I hate to see so many miserable women. But like I tell them time after time, I don't twist anybody's arm to get them to come here. I enjoy my friends' company, but I could do without seeing them so often. Also, I'd be better off financially if I wasn't treating so many of them to free mescal and free late night meals. It'd leave me money to marry Paclita. Yes, marry! But I can't tell my friends anything. I really can't.

What would all these women think if they knew how desperately I wanted to marry Paclita? Would they talk to Paclita and arrange it? If I was married, their husbands probably wouldn't hang out here so much. I can imagine Paclita saying, "What are you bums doing here all the time? You should go home to your wives and children. Or, if you're going to stay here, do some work. Here, take this broom. Sweep the sidewalk. And you, wash the windows. And you, straighten out those shelves. What are you all looking at me for? You want to pour yourselves a drink of mescal? Don't you remember? You drank it all. What do you think we are, made of money? Bring your own bottle if you want to do some drinking. But you'll have to do your drinking in the alley. We can't have customers seeing that sort of thing in the store. It's bad for business." And at closing time I can imagine her chasing my friends away like dogs, "Go home. You're not going to get anything to eat here. Go on home." But what if I told my friends' wives and they laughed in my face? "Such a pretty, innocent girl like her," they'd say, "you should be ashamed of yourself." I'd never hear an end to it.

5

Paclita has stopped going by my store. It's been over a month now. I have to find her. It's getting harder and harder for me to stay put in the store. I find myself closing earlier and earlier. My friends don't understand what's going on. I tried making excuses, but they didn't want any of that. And when the mescal bottle went empty and wasn't replaced by a full one—I'm short of money with the few hours I work and I stopped treating them to midnight meals—they stopped coming by.

The other day I thought I had found Paclita. I was passing through an area of crumbling buildings. It was late afternoon and I was feeling gloomy. Dark clouds were building up for the usual late afternoon shower. For no reason at all, I went through a doorway that opened up into a long abandoned courtyard. The courtyard had several dead or dying trees. A few streaks of light pierced the shadows.

My heart took a jump. It looked like Paclita sitting alone against a low rock wall. She was mostly in shadows, and I noticed that her head was bowed, but when she heard me step on a dry branch, she raised her head.

"Paclita!" I said, my heart pumping furiously. "Paclita, I've been looking for you. I love you, Paclita. I want you to marry me." And then Paclita laughed, a chilling laugh. It was a laughter broken up by coughing. And then I saw the shadow try to stand up. The shadow I had thought was Paclita. As she stood up, a streak of light hit her face, and I saw the worn face of an old woman. She sat back down, still trying to laugh.

"What's the matter with you?" I said, walking closer to her. I didn't want to believe it wasn't Paclita. But I had to get a closer look. I had to know. And as I got very close to her, I could see she was an old woman.

"Are you sick?" I said.

"Yes," she said in a voice so old and cracked it startled me to hear it. It hurt to listen to it. "I'm dying," she said, "and I'm drunk. And nobody cares about me, and I don't care about anybody." And then she burst out laughing again. And I saw her arm move. And I felt something hard hitting my chest. At first

136

I was too shocked to feel any pain. She had thrown something at me. I heard something break. She had thrown a bottle at me, and when it bounced off me, it shattered against a rock. "Paclita," she said in an agonized voice, a parody of a living voice. And then her chilling laughter again. A laughter broken up with coughing, a laughter that was breaking apart as soon as she began it.

"Look. Don't throw things at me," I yelled. I saw her arm move again, and I felt something hit me on the leg. I cursed her. It was beginning to rain. I backed away slowly, ready to duck if her arm moved again. A large bolt of lightning illuminated the courtyard. I could see her in sickening detail. Her eyes were open, and so was her mouth, but she wasn't laughing anymore. Her arms were listless by her sides, her mouth was wide open, and her eyes frightened me with their stony gaze. The rain was pouring down hard. I backed out the doorway and ran down the street. When I stepped out of the rain, I was already blocks away and completely drenched. I wondered if the old woman was dead. I wondered if I should go back when the rain stopped. But then I could still hear her laughter in my mind, her disturbing laughter when I had called her Paclita, a laughter that hurt me as if it had been some physical violence. This upset me greatly. I hoped she was dead. When the rain died down, I didn't think of going back to that courtyard. I rushed to my store, but I didn't open. I sat far back in a corner, and through the front windows, I watched the constant flow of people. And none of them knew I existed. That I was there in the shadows watching them, but not watching them as if they were people. Watching them as if they were memories of no special importance.